SECRET POWERS

SECRET POWERS

SCHOLASTIC INC.

New York   Toronto   London   Auckland   Sydney
Mexico City   New Delhi   Hong Kong   Buenos Aires

Designed by Keirsten Geise

WINX CLUB™ © 2005 Rainbow Srl.

Used under license by Scholastic Inc. All Rights Reserved. Published by Scholastic Inc. SCHOLASTIC and associated logos are trademarks and/or registered trademarks of Scholastic Inc.

ISBN 0-439-68511-7

12 11 10 9 8 7 6 5 4 3 2 1   5 6 7 8 9/0

Printed in the U.S.A.

First printing, February 2005

CHAPTER 1

Bloom couldn't see. She cautiously moved forward in darkness. However, the young girl wasn't frightened at all. She was extremely excited.

"Almost there," her dad said. His hands still covered her eyes.

Bloom carefully shuffled down their front steps. She held her breath. If her surprise was outside, it could only be one thing. After all, her father had told her that it was a little something to help her get around Gardenia. Bloom bit her lower lip.

"We hope you like it," said her mother.

After a few more steps, Bloom's father pulled his hands away from her eyes. Still excited, Bloom kept them shut tightly. Finally, she took a deep breath and opened them. Her breath froze in her throat as she saw what was parked in the driveway. It wasn't the brand-new scooter she had been expecting. Instead, she saw a plain red bicycle. To be fair, it *was* a nice bike. Its front basket even held some fruit and freshly cut flowers. But it was no scooter.

"Nice, huh?" her dad asked. He nervously adjusted his tie.

Bloom looked down at Kiko. Her little gray-and-white bunny chirped and happily twitched his nose. He seemed to like the bike just fine. Bloom thought she should take her cue from Kiko. After all, she didn't want to hurt her parents' feelings.

"It's great," she said, hoping she sounded sincere. She brushed a strand of her long red hair away from her face. "Thanks!" She walked over to check out the bike.

"See," her dad said behind her. "She hardly knew what to say."

"I don't know," her mom whispered. "Maybe she was expecting something a bit more sophisticated."

"A bike with a speedometer?" asked her dad.

"A scooter, Mike," her mother replied.

"But scooters are dangerous, and they cost a bundle," her dad explained.

Bloom sighed. She pretended not to listen as she picked up Kiko and placed him in the basket. Her mom and dad walked back to their house.

"We'll try to put some money aside," said her mom. "Maybe next year we can get her one."

Once they were inside, Bloom climbed on the bike and pedaled out of the driveway. She turned right and headed for the city park.

"Dad won't change, Kiko," she said. "Even though I'm already sixteen, I'll never get to ride anything faster than a bicycle."

Kiko didn't seem to mind one bit. With both paws on the front of the basket, he smiled as his thin whiskers and long ears flapped in the breeze.

Bloom supposed she should be grateful for the new bike. Her parents didn't have a lot of money and even regular bicycles weren't cheap. She shouldn't have gotten her hopes up for a scooter, anyway. Bloom decided that she should stop acting like a brat and be thankful for her gift.

This task was particularly difficult because the bike was just the cherry on top of her real disappointment. It was the first day of vacation and anybody who was *anybody* was going on the school trip to Florida. "But not me," she said to herself. "I'm stuck here pedaling around Gardenia."

As Bloom neared the park, she decided to pull herself together. "Oh, well," she told Kiko. "They say that fun doesn't come from where you are but who you are. And that means you and I are going to have some fun."

Bloom parked her bike in the bike rack. She grabbed Kiko and gently sat him on the ground. The little bunny scampered toward the trees.

"Go find an acorn and I'll toss it to you," she called after him.

As the little rabbit disappeared into the woods, Bloom grabbed an apple from the basket and sat under a tree. She took a bite and began one of her favorite pastimes —

daydreaming. She loved to imagine herself in mystical realms where dragons flew, unicorns galloped, and fairies cast magical spells. In those kingdoms, she wasn't ordinary Bloom Peters who was stuck in her hometown all summer. Bloom imagined herself to be a beautiful fairy princess who fought evil with her magical powers and explored enchanted places.

Bloom was just settling into her daydream when she was suddenly jerked back to reality. Kiko chirped loudly as he ran out of the woods. The little bunny dashed up to her and began tugging at her pant leg.

"What is it, Kiko?" asked Bloom. "Did you see one of those scary squirrels again?"

The small rabbit tugged harder, then ran back toward the trees. Something had obviously spooked him. And whatever it was, he wanted Bloom to check it out. She dropped the apple as she sprang to her feet and chased after him.

Kiko led her down a winding trail that ended at a small clearing. The bunny hopped onto a stump and pointed toward the open area. Bloom ran up to a nearby tree and peeked around its thick trunk. She gasped and her heart pounded. She couldn't believe what she saw!

CHAPTER 2

BAM!

Bloom shielded her face as a flash of light burst from the clearing. When she opened her eyes, she saw a beautiful young girl with flowing blond hair, wearing a sparkling, two-piece outfit with tall, golden boots. A girl like this was odd enough to see in Gardenia. But what really made her stand out was her long staff and the four gleaming wings sprouting from her back.

"Back, ghouls!" the girl shouted.

Even more odd were the three horrible creatures that stood at the other side of the clearing. They looked like a cross between monkeys and crabs. Large claws snapped at the end of each of their four legs. Two short, devil horns budded over their menacing, yellow eyes.

As the monsters loped toward her, the girl raised her staff high into the air. "*Solar Wind Blast!*" she cried as she slammed the staff to the ground. Another burst of brilliant light sent the ghouls flying across the clearing.

"Whoa!" said Bloom as she turned to Kiko. "This has to be a dream!"

If Bloom was dreaming, then it had just turned into a nightmare. A huge beast stomped out of the shadows at the other side of the clearing. The new monster was tall, fat, and wore dirty, brown overalls. It caught one of the flying ghouls with its pudgy, yellow hand. Baring its sharp fangs, the monster squeezed the smaller creature until it burst into a cloud of golden sparkles. As the giant beast moved closer to the young girl, ten more ghouls crawled out of the forest behind it.

"News flash, ogre," yelled the girl as she twirled her staff. "The awesome power of Solaria is so going to flatten you!"

"You're the one who's going to get flattened!" growled the monster. He roared and the ground shook as he bounded toward her.

The girl raised her staff high above her head. On its tip was a large circle with lines jutting toward the center, like the spokes of a wheel. The circle glowed, as it seemed to gather energy for another attack.

Unfortunately, it didn't gather the energy fast enough. The ogre slammed into the much smaller girl. She flew backward and tumbled to a stop on the hard ground.

"That had to hurt," Bloom said to Kiko.

The giant ogre laughed. "You're finished, little fairy girl!" The ghouls surrounded the fallen fairy.

Bloom put a hand to her mouth. "Oh, no!"

"Bring me her scepter, ghouls!" the ogre ordered.

The ghouls hissed as they pounced on the young girl. She struggled as their claws clamped on to her legs, arms, and neck. Two of them latched on to the scepter and wrenched it from her hands. They scampered over to the ogre and presented their prize.

The blond girl struggled against the creatures. "You'll never get away with this!" she cried.

The ogre examined the long staff and chuckled. "I think I just did." He raised it high above his head in triumph. "The scepter is ours!" He aimed it toward the girl. "And you're history."

Then something unexpected happened. As if watching herself in a dream, Bloom could feel herself step into the clearing. She knew that there was nothing she could do to help the poor girl, but she moved forward, anyway. Somehow it just happened. Worst of all, she heard her own voice as she yelled at the horrible beasts. "Leave her alone!" she cried. "And come get me!"

Each of the creatures snapped its head toward Bloom and snarled. Bloom's eyes widened, and she slammed a hand over her mouth. "Wait a minute. Did I just say that?"

"You sure did," said the large ogre through a wide grin. "You should learn to mind your own business." He pointed a finger at Bloom and three of the smaller ghouls galloped after her.

Bloom didn't know what to do. The other girl had a magical scepter and *she* couldn't defeat these monsters.

Oddly enough, however, Bloom wasn't frightened. Even though she knew she should be terrified, a warm calm washed over her. In fact, it did more than wash; it seemed to burn in her veins.

As the first beast leaped toward her, Bloom raised one hand. "Get back!" she ordered. Her entire body glowed and a golden sphere formed around her. All three ghouls slammed against the shimmering ball and convulsed as if they were being filled with electricity. Then they burst into wisps of tiny sparkles.

Bloom looked down at her hand. "What just happened?" she asked. "How did I do that?"

Still standing on the stump beside her, Kiko cheered. He danced around and pretended to box like a prizefighter. Just then, a ghoul snuck up behind him. It was about to grab the bunny with its sharp claw.

"Hey, ghoul," said Bloom as she picked up a large stick. "Back off!" She batted the ghoul away from Kiko. It sailed across the forest, slammed into a tree, and evaporated into a puff of sparkles.

Bloom's attention was so focused on saving her bunny that she hadn't seen the giant ogre lumber toward her. He snatched her up by both arms. "What have we here?" he asked as he hoisted her high above his head.

Once again, Bloom felt something burn inside her. She closed her eyes and imagined magical flames washing over her entire body. "Noooooo!" she yelled as her body glowed brighter than before.

WHAM!

Brilliant golden light seemed to explode from every pore of her skin. The ogre released her arms just before being blasted backward. Bloom hovered in midair as the bright light snaked around her. Finally, it shot into the afternoon sky and exploded in a fiery burst brighter than any fireworks display.

Bloom crumpled to the ground. The ogre and all the remaining ghouls were already flattened on the ground around her. They moaned in pain as they passed in and out of consciousness.

Bloom was a little light-headed, but she made it to her feet. She stared at her hands in disbelief. She had no idea what had just happened. Bloom looked at Kiko, who stared at her with equal bewilderment.

"Wow," said the blond girl as she got to her feet. "You've got major Winx, girl!"

"Me?" asked Bloom. "What do you mean?"

The ogre groaned as he crawled toward the dropped scepter. As one of his chunky hands reached for it, the girl snatched it away from him.

"Look here, you fashion fiasco," she said as she aimed the scepter at the beast. "I suggest you get out of this realm now!"

Bloom saw several of the ghouls awaken and creep toward the girl. "Watch out!" she warned.

The blond fairy spun the long scepter over her head as if it were a golden twirling baton. It glowed brightly as she

9

stopped it, then slashed the air in front of her. The red ghouls flew backward and landed in a neat pile. All at once, they sparkled away like the others. The fairy planted the staff beside her and stood proudly.

She didn't finish off *all* the ghouls, however. One snuck up to Bloom and bit her pant leg. "Get off!" Bloom yelled, kicking at the creature. Her pant leg ripped as her foot connected with its forehead. The little monster tumbled away with a piece of cloth in its slimy mouth. Once it regained its footing, the ghoul scampered over to the ogre.

"We'll meet again, Princess Stella!" yelled the ogre. He clapped his hands together dramatically. Suddenly, he and the few remaining ghouls disappeared in a flash of purple light.

"I can't say I'm looking forward to *that*," Stella smirked.

Bloom was about to ask what was going on when the princess suddenly clutched her staff with both hands. She tried to hold herself up but couldn't. Her knees buckled and she collapsed.

"Oh, no!" cried Bloom. "Are you okay?"

Bloom ran and knelt beside her. The mysterious girl was still breathing but was out cold. Bloom was so worried that she hardly noticed the fairy's outfit transforming to a simple dress. Her wings disappeared and her scepter shrank and morphed into a small ring on her finger. Kiko hopped up to the unconscious, and more normal-looking, girl.

"We better take her home!" Bloom told him. "She needs major help!"

CHAPTER 3

Bloom slowly woke the next morning. She lay there with her eyes closed, listening to Kiko snore in his basket beside her bed. A small smile crept across her face. She had just had the strangest dream. She dreamed that she had met a beautiful fairy in the woods. However, this fairy didn't just have good looks — she packed a powerful punch as well. She fought off a giant ogre and several ugly little ghouls. And in her dream, Bloom had special powers, too! It was the weirdest thing.

She heard her mother enter the room. "Rise and shine, princess," her mother said. "A beautiful day awaits!"

Bloom sat up and stretched as her mother opened the curtains. The rays of the morning sun danced over her room — a room that very much resembled her dreams. Her walls were covered with drawings of fairies, castles, and dragons. Bloom scanned the pictures to see if one of them looked like the girl in her dream. None of them did.

The girl in her dream didn't resemble the stereotypical fairy — a pointy-eared pixie with butterfly wings. The blond fairy princess looked like a beautiful young woman not much older than Bloom herself. She couldn't wait to tell her mom all about her crazy dream.

"By the way," said her mother, "who's the girl asleep in the guest room?"

"What?" asked Bloom. Her eyes sprang open. She was suddenly wide awake. It wasn't a dream after all. "Um," Bloom stammered. "She's a friend from out of town." Bloom didn't think that was far from the truth. "Way, *way* out of town."

"I've never met her before," her mom said.

"Uh, she's a new friend," Bloom said as she ran to the bathroom. "Don't wake her yet, okay?"

"Okay," her mom replied as she headed for the door. "Just come and introduce us when you're ready."

Bloom showered and dried her hair as fast as she could. However, her body wasn't racing nearly as fast as her mind. How was she really going to explain having a fairy princess spend the night? And what about her battle in the park? If it wasn't a dream, then Bloom really did have magical powers. But how could that be?

Bloom pulled on a fresh pair of jeans and a shirt and practically bounded down the stairs. Her mom and dad sat at the breakfast table. There was no getting past them. She had wanted to ask the girl some questions before she had

12

to answer any of her own. However, it didn't look as if that would happen.

"In a big hurry to help me clean out the garage, huh?" her dad asked.

"Come on, Dad," Bloom replied. "I have lots of other stuff to do. Lots of important stuff."

"That's right, Mike," her mom agreed. "She has a friend over, remember?"

"Yes, why don't you tell us about this friend?" asked Mr. Peters. He pulled out the chair beside him and slapped the seat.

It was no use; she was trapped. Bloom blew a strand of red hair from her face and plopped into the awaiting chair. For a second, she tried to think of a cover story. Bloom had never really lied to her parents, so it didn't come easy. She thought harder, but still nothing. She supposed, as always, the truth would be the best way to go. Of course, if they locked her away in an insane asylum afterward, at least she could take comfort in the fact that she had told the truth. *Great,* Bloom thought. *Not much comfort there.*

"Well?" her dad asked.

Bloom nervously twirled a strand of hair. "Do you remember when I was *really* into fairies and witches?"

"Of course," her father answered.

"You were always so cute pretending to know magic," said Mrs. Peters.

"Well, here's the thing—" Bloom started.

"In fact," her dad interrupted, "if you knew magic, you could just wave a wand, and the garage would clean itself!"

Bloom put her head in her hands. This wasn't going to be easy.

CHAPTER 4

Knut ambled into the large chamber. All around him was darkness except for the single shaft of light in which he stood. He nervously wrung his large yellow hands. He didn't know how he was going to explain this one. No one would ever believe that a great big ogre like himself could be defeated by a little girl. She wasn't even a fairy. She definitely had magical powers, though. They were stronger than any fairy magic he'd ever seen.

"Well, look who's failed us again," said a shrill voice.

Knut looked up to see three giant pairs of eyes glaring down at him. Sometimes the three witches projected menacing images of themselves for intimidation. They had portrayed themselves as giant serpents, hungry tigers, and menacing hawks. Today seemed to be "giant eyeball" day. Knut wasn't really intimidated by these illusions anymore. But he wouldn't dare tell that to Icy, Darcy, or Stormy.

"Explain yourself, Knut!" Icy ordered. She was the

leader of the three witches and usually did most of the yelling.

"It really wasn't my fault this time, Your Wickedness!" Knut pleaded. "The scepter was mine. I had it in my hand!"

"But —" said Icy.

Knut lowered his head. "But then this Earth girl attacked me."

"Wait a minute," said Darcy. "He didn't just say *Earth* girl, did he?"

"Yeah, but this was no ordinary girl," Knut explained. "She had powerful magic. She basically took us on with one hand!"

"What did she look like?" asked Stormy.

Knut scratched his head. "I'm, uh ... not sure."

"Where are your glasses?" asked Icy.

Knut reached into his overalls and pulled out his glasses. The two clunky, square lenses were held by thick, oversized frames. "Here, Your Wickedness."

"Knut!" Icy boomed. The ground shook beneath the ogre's feet. "How many times do we have to tell you? You are *never* to remove your glasses!"

Knut quickly put them on.

"Don't you know you're as blind as a hairless mole rat without them?" asked Darcy. "You buffoon!"

"I don't like these frames," said Knut. "They're not ... *me*."

"Silence!" Icy roared. "We must find this girl!"

Knut smiled. "I already have a plan!"

"Go on," Icy coaxed. She sounded intrigued.

Knut reached into a pocket and pulled out a small piece of denim. "One of my ghouls grabbed this." He held up the scrap. "It's a piece of the Earth girl's clothing!"

Knut turned and waved the fabric at the darkness beside him. The ground shook once more as a giant troll tromped into view. Its long greasy black hair stuck to its slimy blue skin. "All I have to do is give it to this hunter troll and he can track her down!" Knut continued.

The troll snatched the cloth out of Knut's hand. It smelled the fabric and grinned a crooked smile.

"Very well," said Icy. "Go and find this meddling Earth girl."

"Right!" said Knut as he gave a quick salute.

"If she's still with that fairy," Icy continued, "destroy them both and bring me that scepter!"

CHAPTER 5

"So you're saying this girl in our guest room is a fairy?" Bloom's father asked. "Is that like a Goth thing or something?" Both he and Bloom's mother stared at her from across the table.

"I mean she's a *real* fairy, Dad," Bloom explained. "With a scepter, magic powers, fluttering wings…everything!"

Bloom's mom just stared at her. Her dad stood and paced (for the fifth time). After an uncomfortable silence, he finally spoke. "You must have a very high fever. I think we should call Doctor Silverman." He snatched the cordless from its base on the shelf.

"Now, Mike," said her mom.

Just then, the fairy in question walked into the room. "Good morning," she chirped.

"Good morning," said Bloom's mom. "How do you feel?"

"Fine now." She put an arm around Bloom. "Thanks to this girl right here!"

"It was nothing," said Bloom. "Really."

The girl grabbed Bloom's hand. "My name is Stella, by the way."

"My name is Bloom Peters," Bloom replied, shaking the girl's hand.

Bloom's mother stood and took the cordless phone from Mr. Peters' hand. "Let's call your parents, Stella," she said. "Shall we?"

Stella giggled. "I'm afraid that's way easier said than done." She pointed toward the ceiling. "I mean, let's face it, they live six whole realms away! In a kingdom called Solaria!" She turned back to Bloom. "I was on my way to Alfea, you know, to continue my magic training...."

Mr. Peters grabbed the phone back from Bloom's mom. "Oh boy, oh boy," he said. "I'm calling Doctor Silverman. We'll see if he can figure out why the two of you are seeing things that aren't there."

"You mean seeing things like this?" asked Stella. She aimed a finger at Mr. Peters. A beam of sparkling light shot from her fingertip and hit the phone in his hand. With a flash of light and a puff of smoke, the phone changed into a carrot.

"Do you still think we're out of our gourds?" asked Stella.

Bloom's dad carefully placed the carrot onto the phone's base. Then he and Mrs. Peters stared at Stella with their mouths wide open.

"Whoa, that was so awesome!" said Bloom.

"You're the one who's awesome, Bloom," Stella replied. She turned to Bloom's awestruck parents. "When this ogre attacked me, Bloom gave him an energy blast that kicked his booty all the way to another dimension!"

Bloom looked at her shocked parents. "It's true, but I don't know how I did it."

"It's like I told you yesterday," said Stella. "You're loaded with magic!"

"Me?" asked Bloom.

Stella snapped her fingers. "Hey, I just got a great brainstorm! You should come to Alfea with me. It's the best magic school in the whole eight-realm area!"

"What?" Bloom's dad asked. "My daughter? Going to another realm?"

Meanwhile, at the abandoned airport across town, lightning roared and litter spun in a whirlwind. Electricity filled the air as Knut appeared in a bright flash of purple light. The ogre wasn't alone, however. The tall, tracking troll appeared at his side. Several snarling ghouls appeared around them both.

"Here we are," said Knut. He immediately took off his glasses and shoved them into his dirty overalls. He pulled out the piece of cloth and passed it to the blue beast beside him. "Troll, do your thing!"

The ugly troll inhaled deeply as it smelled the scrap from the girl's pant leg. Then it lifted its slimy blue nose toward the sky. It carefully sniffed the air in all directions. "Girl very close," it growled.

The troll began to lumber toward the girl's scent. It led the way as the group of creatures marched out of the airport and toward the other side of Gardenia.

Knut smiled, baring his yellow fangs. With fresh ghouls and the unbridled power of the huge troll, he knew he couldn't fail.

CHAPTER 6

Back at her house, Bloom led Stella into her bedroom. She needed to give her parents some time to digest everything they had told them. It's not every day you meet a real fairy. Not to mention discovering that your only daughter has magical powers, too.

Kiko hopped out of his bed and greeted them as they entered. The fairy princess knelt and stroked his soft fur as she gazed at the colorful room.

"Cool room, Bloom!" she said. She stood and put a hand to her chin. "You should bring it to Alfea! I have a quick packing spell that will fit it all in a single handbag."

"Stella, I don't think I'm going to Alfea," Bloom said with a sigh. "I don't even know if I have powers anymore." She sat on the edge of her bed. "I mean, I know I fought that ogre in the park, but I don't feel very powerful now."

"Trust me, Bloom," Stella said as she placed a hand on Bloom's shoulder. "Someone with magic like yours doesn't lose her powers. They're just rusty from sitting unused for so long."

Stella wandered over to the bookshelf and picked up a book about mystical realms, wizards, and fairies. She thumbed through the pages then stopped on one with an illustration of a beautiful fairy. The tiny pixie was casting a spell at a fire-breathing dragon. Bloom stood and looked over her shoulder.

"Do you think I'm like the girl in that book?" asked Bloom.

"Kind of," Stella said with a chuckle. "But this book was written by humans." She pointed to the fairy's dress of leaves and vines. "You're *much* more fashionable."

Bloom giggled, then gazed at her own hands. "It's still hard to believe that I really know magic." She cocked her head. "And what did you call it? Winx?"

"That's right," said Stella. She slid the book back between two others on a shelf. "Your magic has always been inside you. It's just like my fairy godmother used to say....Sometimes you need an ogre attack to find out what you're really made of."

Stella looked at Bloom's desk and raised a hand. "Now, try this. It's a simple matter-merger exercise." Stella pointed to a cup of pencils. A glittering beam erupted from her fingertip and struck the cup. The cup jumped and the pencils rose into the air. They swirled around for a moment and then morphed into one giant pencil.

The pencil continued to hover as Stella crossed her arms. "Okay, you give it a shot," Stella suggested. "Put them back the way they were."

Bloom pointed at the large, floating pencil. She imagined a similar beam shooting from her fingertip but nothing happened. She tried again, closing her eyes and visualizing the pencils the way they were. The large pencil continued to hang just below her ceiling.

"Come on, try again," said Stella.

Bloom put both hands in front of her and closed her eyes. She focused all her thoughts on the floating pencil. This time, she felt something happen. She opened her eyes just in time to see it wobble, then drop to the ground. It didn't change at all.

Bloom sighed. "I don't feel any powers." She plopped onto her bed.

"You just need some practice." Stella zapped the large pencil once more. "It's really no biggie." The pencil shot off the ground, spun around near the ceiling, and split into the five original pencils. They gently slipped back into the cup on Bloom's desk.

"That's why you *have* to come with me to Alfea!" Stella sat down beside Bloom. "Before long, you'll be zapping ogres left and right!"

"So where is this place?" asked Bloom.

"Well, it's sort of in a parallel dimension," Stella explained. "You go to the inner realm of the enchanted ring and then you…" She thought for a moment. "Look, just come with me and I'll show it to you!"

Stella held out a hand and a small postcard appeared. It showed a photo of a grand castle nestled inside a beautiful forest. "This is an express portal," she said.

Stella threw the postcard onto the floor, and it expanded to the size of a large rug. "Come on. It's cool," Stella said as she stepped onto the giant picture. When she did, the surface began to ripple like water. Stella slowly began to sink into the image. "Just follow me!"

After Stella dropped below the surface, Bloom timidly stepped onto the portal. She, too, began to sink. "This feels really weird," she said.

"Don't worry," Stella's voice came from below her. "Almost no one gets lost between dimensions."

Almost *no one?* Bloom thought, as her head slipped into the rippling portal.

When Bloom was all the way through, she dropped a few feet to land on soft grass. Now standing in a forest, Bloom looked up to see her bedroom through a shimmering rectangle above her. The image rippled as if she were looking up from the bottom of a swimming pool.

"Well, there it is!" Stella announced as she pointed to the horizon. "The famous Alfea School for Fairies!"

Just beyond the trees, a sparkling castle sat on a lush, green hill. Birds serenely soared past glistening, pink towers with tiny blue windows. Smaller buildings huddled inside a tall, circling wall. Two large gates, resembling fairy wings, guarded the entrance to the beautiful school grounds.

"So what exactly goes on there?" asked Bloom.

"The best and the most fabulous girls come from all over the universe to perfect their powers," Stella replied. "Some are princesses like me, but we also have pixies and gwillions." She pointed in the opposite direction. "And get this — we're only *one* enchanted forest away from the Red Fountain School for Heroics and Bravery." She smiled and bit her lower lip. "It's full of hunks!"

Bloom could just make out the tip of a red tower over the treetops. Stella turned and pointed in a third direction. The clouds on that horizon were dark and buzzing with flashes of lightning. "We're also just down the lagoon from the creepiest place in the entire realm — the Cloud Tower School for Witches."

Bloom didn't know what to think. She was excited just standing in this enchanted land — a *real* enchanted land, not one from her books or her daydreams. But she was also a bit frightened. "This is a really big decision," she said.

Stella shot her a sly smile. "To help make up your mind, I invited some of the Red Fountain boys over to your house to meet you."

Bloom gasped. "The hero guys are coming to my house? When?"

"Pretty soon!" Stella said with a laugh. "So let's get

going!" She sprang into the air and shot right through the portal above.

Bloom did the same. To her surprise, she flew straight up and splashed into the rippling image of her room. She slowly rose out of the giant postcard and was once again in her room.

Bloom was back in her world, in her own bedroom, in her own reality. She didn't feel any more at ease, however. She knew that she had a really big choice to make. A choice that could change her life forever.

CHAPTER 7

While Stella stayed upstairs, Bloom sat in the living room with her parents. She had been trying to convince them to let her go to Alfea, but it wasn't an easy task. Going to a different school was one thing. Going to an entirely different realm was another.

"I don't know, Bloom," said her dad. "A young girl turns up, shows us a quick magic trick, and now I'm supposed to believe in fairies?"

"If you had only seen her at the park," Bloom explained. "If you saw how she fought that ogre — how *we* fought that ogre, you'd be totally convinced."

"You have to admit, dear," said Mrs. Peters. "It is a bit hard to swallow. We don't have as big an imagination as you do."

Bloom crossed her arms. "I'm not imagining anything. It all really happened!"

Suddenly, Kiko ran into the room. He grabbed Mr.

Peters's pant leg with one paw and pointed to the kitchen with the other.

"Not now, Kiko!" said Bloom's dad. "We can play later!"

"I don't know what's wrong with him," said Bloom's mom. She turned to her daughter. "Did you forget to feed him?"

"Maybe he's doing that thing where he pretends he didn't eat so he can get a second serving," Mr. Peters suggested.

Bloom leaned over. "What is it, Kiko?" But Kiko only ran up to her, chirped one more time, then hid behind her chair.

"I told you we should have bought you a hamster!" Mr. Peters barked.

CRASH!

The kitchen door shattered and in stepped a monster more hideous than the ogre at the park. The door frame cracked as he squeezed inside. He roared and slammed a giant blue fist on the kitchen table. A pile of splinters was all that was left.

"That thing is repulsive!" said Bloom's mom.

"And angry!" her dad added.

"*Now* do you believe me?" asked Bloom.

The three of them stepped back as more monsters entered their formerly peaceful home. Several red ghouls crawled in and sprang to all parts of the kitchen. They began breaking dishes and tearing down cabinets. Bloom's dad held up a pillow to block of few of the plates flying their way.

Finally, the yellow ogre from the park stepped through the doorway. "There you are!" he bellowed. "Tell us where your friend is or you're ghoul food!"

"Turn around, Sunshine!" said a voice behind Bloom. She whipped around and saw Stella standing at the bottom of the staircase.

"Aha!" the ogre cried.

"I guess you didn't learn your lesson, did you, Knut?" Stella taunted. She closed her eyes and raised a fist into the air. "*Sun Power!*"

Stella's ring glowed brightly as she rose into the air. She extended the first two fingers of each hand then crossed her arms. Suddenly, her flowing dress shifted into the golden shorts and top she had worn the day before. Tall, sparkling boots appeared on her feet and gold bracelets materialized on her arms. Stella arched her back and four small fairy wings sprouted.

When Stella was fully transformed, she flew toward the troll. Her wings fluttered madly as she landed a kick on his chest. The blue beast stumbled back a few feet but quickly recovered.

"You just going to stand there and let that little fairy kick your butt?" asked Knut.

The troll straightened and growled, "Me mad!"

"Then do something about it, tall, blue, and gruesome!" Stella teased.

The two giants stomped forward as the ghouls surrounded the girls and Bloom's parents, blocking the front door.

"Let's get out of here," said Mr. Peters. He opened the window and helped Mrs. Peters climb out. He quickly followed her then reached a hand out for Bloom. "Come on!"

She ignored his offer. She didn't know how to use her powers, but she wasn't going to abandon her new friend. She stood her ground beside Stella.

"I'll handle the two gross-outs," Stella told her. "You take care of the ghouls."

"How?" asked Bloom.

Stella smiled and winked. "You'll think of something."

"Okay, I'll try." Bloom hopped over the nearest ghoul and ran to the front door. She threw it open and dashed outside. Most of the ghouls raced after her.

Once outside, she could still hear the taunting ogre. "Now that her friend's gone, she doesn't stand a chance!" he told the troll. "It's time to make some fairy dust!"

"Bring it on!" Stella yelled back at him. "I'm going to whoop you and not even muss my hair!"

Bloom turned her attention away from the crashes inside the house. She had her own little problem at hand — actually, *four* little problems with very sharp claws. The ghouls hissed as they inched closer. They remained in a cautious group, but they looked as if they could attack at any moment.

Bloom focused, but she didn't feel any powers emerging.

She even pointed to the ghouls and concentrated on turning them into a giant pencil. Still nothing.

Bloom gave a nervous giggle. "Uh, nice little poochies," she said. "Roll over?"

Just then, a large stew pot shot out of the door and slid, facedown, along the sidewalk. It swerved around the ghouls and headed straight for Bloom. After it ran into her shoes, she picked it up and saw that Kiko was hiding underneath. Apparently, he had found his own way out of their battle zone of a house. The little rabbit zipped toward Bloom's parents, who were standing on the sidewalk.

The ghouls crept closer, and Bloom had to think of something fast. Then she heard a loud noise from inside her house.

SMACK!

The giant ogre flew through the front door and landed on the ghouls in front of her. Bloom's four problems were suddenly solved. "Good one, Stella!" she called out.

SMACK-SMACK-CRASH!

This time, Stella flew out of the house, crashing through the front window.

"Oh, no!" Bloom cried as she raced to her friend.

Stella seemed a bit shaken, but she was already starting to sit up. As Bloom knelt beside her, the hideous troll squeezed through the front door, fracturing the frame around him. It didn't waste any time. The beast rounded on Bloom and Stella.

"What do we do?" Bloom asked.

CHAPTER 8

As the troll reached out to grab them, a black line came out of nowhere and wrapped around its neck. The troll was heaved backward and the two girls were able to shuffle out of arm's reach.

"Hey, Princess Stella," a voice said. "I hope your friend is the pretty one with red hair and not this ugly guy at the end of the leash here!"

Four young boys now stood in Bloom's yard. They each wore blue-and-white uniforms with flowing blue capes. Three were armed with swords and other weapons Bloom didn't recognize. One held the end of the whip wrapped around the troll's neck.

"Those are the Red Fountain boys I told you about," Stella explained. "That's Brandon, Sky, Riven, and Timmy."

"I say we do a three-prong rescue op," Brandon suggested. He shook his blond hair out of his face and held his sword and shield ready.

"Forget that," said Riven as he held tight to the end of the whip. "I got this puppy wrapped up all by myself."

Sky leaned against his large green sword and flicked a strand of his black hair away from his eyes. He actually seemed bored. "Dude, one summer at swashbuckler camp doesn't mean you can go solo on a troll."

"No kidding," agreed Timmy as he adjusted his thin glasses. The youngest of the four held some sort of futuristic ray gun.

The troll grabbed the whip and jerked hard. Riven flew over the monster's head and landed between Bloom and Stella.

Sky smirked. "I rest my case."

"Stay behind me!" ordered Brandon. He held up his shield as the troll charged. The beast pounded on the shield with its giant blue fists, but Brandon held his ground. "What did we learn about battling trolls?" he asked the others.

Sky raised his sword high above his head. "Smash 'em, I think." He slammed his sword onto the ground. The ground split and a giant crack formed between the troll's legs. The angry beast stopped his attack and teetered, trying not to fall into the chasm.

"That's not it," Timmy corrected. He aimed his strange gun at the troll. "We're supposed to take out their feet!"

He fired the weapon and three glowing arrows flew toward the chasm. They sparkled and zigzagged like fireflies until they smashed into the ground below the troll's feet. The earth exploded, and the monster fell into the dark ravine.

"Good one, Timmy!" said Sky.

"Very nice," complimented Brandon.

"It's a good thing he paid attention in Intro to Forest Creatures class," said Sky.

One beast was down, but there were several others to deal with. The ogre roared as several more ghouls charged the two girls.

"Stay here," Riven told them. "This won't take long."

He drew a slender sword and slashed at the ghouls. With each swipe, they bounded out of the way just in time. While Riven was distracted, the ogre charged and slapped him away.

"Leave him alone!" Bloom yelled as she thrust her hands forward. To her surprise, a burst of gold light shot from her hands and hit the ogre square in the back. The creature flew forward and skidded across the yard.

"Awesome shot there, Bloom," said Stella.

Bloom examined her hands. "It just happened." She glanced at her mother and father. They stared at her with amazement.

Stella put a hand on her shoulder. "Like I said, you got Winx!"

The ogre slowly stood to find himself surrounded by Bloom, Stella, and the boys from Red Fountain. The remaining ghouls quickly scurried to him and clambered for protection.

"I'm going to put my *Stinkus Removus* spell on him," Stella announced as she raised her hands. "He's going to end up smelling like he just took a bath!"

The ogre closed his eyes and clapped his hands together. Just as before, he and the ghouls disappeared in a flash of purple light.

Stella chuckled. "I knew that would scare him." She turned to the boys. "Guys, this is Bloom. She's the one I told you about."

As the boys greeted Bloom, the tracking troll poked his head out of the chasm. Timmy noticed it and reached behind his back. He pulled out a glowing ring and opened it. "Not so fast, tough guy!" He snapped the ring around the troll's neck. "You better come with us!" The ring created two electric tendrils that wrapped around the beast. It rose out of the chasm and hovered a few feet off the ground.

"Yeah, you've done enough damage for one day, pal," said Sky.

"Where are you guys taking him?" asked Bloom.

"We'll take him back to Red Fountain," said Brandon. "They'll probably send him to a creature preserve."

Timmy pulled out a small remote and pressed a button. The air felt charged as a whirlwind of light formed in front of the boys and the captured troll. Bloom could just make out a forest beyond the churning vortex.

"So long," said Sky.

"Bye," said Timmy. "Nice meeting you."

"Good-bye," said Bloom, "and thanks!"

As the boys stepped through the portal, Brandon stopped and looked back. His long blond hair swirled around his face, and he looked at her with his pale blue eyes. "I sure hope I see you at Alfea, Bloom," he said.

Bloom caught her breath in her throat. Of all the Red Fountain boys, she thought Brandon was the cutest. "Me, too," she said with a smile and a big wave. Thinking she was acting like a total goof, she quickly put her hand down. She felt heat rise to her cheeks and knew she was blushing.

Brandon waved back and stepped through the portal. It swirled once more then disappeared with a loud slurp. The neighborhood was quiet once more.

"Well," said Bloom's dad, breaking the silence. "I'm glad *that's* over!"

Chapter 9

The next morning, Bloom and Stella ran down the stairs. Bloom carried her big red suitcase and Kiko hopped down alongside them. Bloom was all packed and ready for school. When they reached the bottom, they saw her dad sweeping up broken dishes from the battle the night before.

"Mr. P, why don't you let me whip this place into shape with a little magic?" asked Stella.

"I've had enough magic, thank you very much!" Bloom's dad replied.

Bloom stepped out from behind Stella, revealing her suitcase. "I'm ready, Dad."

Mr. Peters stopped sweeping. "How come you have a suitcase?"

"You know," said Bloom, "just in case you guys say I can stay. Then I'll be all packed."

Her father leaned the broom against the couch and put an arm around Bloom. "I know that you're way more grown up than we thought you were," he said. "And that you have a special gift, but we still have to check the school out. I mean, we don't have any information about Alfea."

Bloom's mom entered the living room. "But if it's anything like what Stella says it is, you will be in for a wonderful adventure." She clapped her hands together. "This is so exciting!"

"Hey, Stella," said Mr. Peters. "How do we get there? Car? Phone? Broomstick? Do they make a broomstick for four?"

"Um, Dad," said Bloom. "Broomsticks are for witches."

"Oh, yeah. Right," said Mr. Peters. He grabbed his jacket from a hook by what was left of the front door. "So what do you use, Stella? Wait, don't tell me. Is it fairy dust?"

"Are we going to use the portal?" asked Bloom.

"Regular humans can't go through the portal," Stella explained. She took off her ring and held it up. "But my scepter can handle a little trans-dimensional puddle jump like this." She threw her ring up and it magically stretched into the scepter.

Stella plucked the long staff from the air and raised it high over her head. "*Sun Power!*" She brought the end down on the floor, and a purple glow formed around it. The light spread across the floor and up the walls until the room around them seemed to fade out of existence.

Then they were falling.

Stella, Bloom, her parents, and Kiko fell through purple nothingness. They tumbled down until Bloom saw a

39

small portal below. Through the opening, she could make out the familiar forest below.

They dropped through the gateway and gently landed on soft, green grass. Bloom smiled as she saw the amazed expressions on her parents' faces.

"Wow!" her dad said. "Would you look at this place?!"

"Pretty cool, right?" Bloom asked.

"With a capital C," Stella added.

Bloom's mother pointed to the pink castle on the hill. "Is that it?"

"That's it!" announced Stella. "The realm-renowned Alfea School for Fairies!"

"It's amazing!" said Mrs. Peters.

"Wow!" said Mr. Peters.

"Wow, indeed!" said Bloom. "It sure makes public school look lame."

Stella led the way as they trekked across an open field on their way to the towering castle.

"I can't wait to see what it's like!" said Bloom's mom.

"I'm so excited!" said Bloom.

Mr. Peters scratched his head. "I wonder what their policy is for admissions and such."

As they neared the front gate, Bloom saw many other girls walking through the forest toward the castle. They each carried suitcases as they filed through the main archway. Were they *all* fairies?

"Ouch!" Mr. Peters said behind them.

Bloom turned to see her father sitting on the ground,

holding his head. "It's as if there's an invisible wall or something," he said.

Bloom walked back to him as he stood. He reached out and placed his hand on something solid in front of him. "I can't get through it!"

"No?" asked Bloom as she reached for the same place he was touching. "Where is it? I can't feel anything." There was nothing there.

Stella put her hands to her mouth. "I forgot. There actually *is* an invisible wall." With a flick of her wrist, she threw a handful of golden sparkles into the air. They hit the invisible wall, then spread to reveal a giant dome covering all of Alfea.

"It didn't stop me," said Bloom. She pointed to her parents. "Why can't they get through?"

"Simple," said Stella. "You're a magical being, my dear. This barrier keeps out all non-magical creatures."

Bloom walked back through the barrier toward her parents. If her dad couldn't check out the school, would he still let her go? She looked at them and bit her lower lip. "So, what do you think?"

For a moment, neither one of her parents said anything. Then her mom threw her arms around her. "I think you're going to have a great year."

"I'm going to miss you," Bloom said as she felt her eyes tearing up. She and her mom quit hugging and they both turned to her dad.

He reached out and touched the barrier again. He

looked at the castle and shook his head. Then he turned to Bloom. "All right," he finally said. "You can go." Bloom dropped her suitcase and gave him a giant hug. "But try not to run into any more of those…whatever they were," he warned. "Okay?"

Bloom laughed. "I'll do my best!"

Mrs. Peters wiped a tear from her eye. "You're going to have a wonderful time."

"She sure will," Stella reassured. "I'll see to it!"

Bloom walked back through the barrier and Kiko followed her. For some reason, he could pass through as well.

"Kiko," said Mr. Peters, "you keep an eye on her, okay?"

The little rabbit chirped and twitched his nose.

"We should get going," said Stella. She turned back to Bloom's parents. "I'll send you back first-class! Stay there and don't move." Stella twirled her scepter. *Transport-am Back Homus!*" she said, then swiped the long staff over their heads. The two slowly faded away.

"See you later," Bloom yelled. They both waved until they faded out of sight.

Once they were safely transported home, Stella tossed her scepter high into the air. It twirled twice before it shrunk back into the tiny ring. She caught it and placed it back on her finger.

"Come on," said Stella as she pranced toward the main gate. "It's time to make an entrance!"

CHAPTER 10

Kiko hopped along the perfectly manicured grass as the two girls walked toward the front gate. When they reached it, the giant fairy wings slid open and they entered.

There were tons of other girls there, and they all looked so different. Bloom thought they must have been from all over the world. Then she had to remind herself that they weren't even *on* her world anymore. These girls were from all over ... well ... the universe!

"I have butterflies in my stomach," she told Stella.

"Relax, you're here with me," Stella replied. "Besides, fairy school is just like normal school, except we all have magic powers and much better outfits. You'll love it."

Bloom gazed at the giant towers overlooking the vast courtyard. "I'm loving it already!"

Bloom picked up Kiko as the two girls fell into a long line of girls leading to one of the teachers. "Well, you're definitely *not* going to love her," said Stella. She pointed to the older woman at the head of the line. The woman tapped a bony finger on her clipboard as she inspected the girls over her thin, pointed glasses. Either none of the girls met with her approval or the woman had a permanent scowl stretched across her face.

"Who is she?" asked Bloom. "She looks scary."

"That's Griselda, the head of discipline," Stella replied. "She *is* scary and in desperate need of a makeover!"

As the two made their way up the line, Bloom began to make out what Miss Griselda was saying. "First name and place of origin?" the woman asked a young girl.

"Uh…Eleanor of Dolona," a girl answered in a shaky voice. "I signed up online. My name should be on the list."

The old woman scrunched up her nose as she examined her clipboard. "I don't see it," she snapped. "Do you know what happens if you're not on the list? We turn you into a…"

"It's spelled with only one *L*," Eleanor interrupted.

The woman peered at her clipboard once more. "There you are!" she said. "Eleanor of Dolona. You may come in."

"Thank you," said Eleanor. She picked up her suitcase and shuffled toward the main entrance. The lined inched forward.

"Next!" shouted Miss Griselda.

Bloom's heart pounded. "I'm not going to be on the list," she whispered to Stella.

"Fret not," her new friend assured here. "I got it all figured out. The Princess of Vallisto was supposed to come

44

here this year, but she's doing the home-school thing instead." Stella held out a hand and a pink envelope appeared. "She gave me this letter to give to the headmistress." Stella tore the letter to pieces. "I just won't give it to her, and we'll be all set. No one here knows what she looks like, so it's perfect."

"You want me to pretend to be this princess?" Bloom asked. "I don't know. I hate lying."

"We're not lying," Stella whispered. They were almost at the head of the line. "We're just not telling all we know." She winked at Bloom as they stepped up to Miss Griselda.

"Long time no see, Miss G!" Stella said cockily.

"Not long enough, Princess Stella," Miss Griselda barked. "Not after your little *incident* last year." She looked down at her list. "How your parents ever convinced the school board to take you back is completely beyond me."

Stella smiled and twirled a strand of her long, blond hair. "They *did* donate that new computer lab."

Miss Griselda ignored Stella's response. "Who is your friend?" She stared at Bloom over the rims of her glasses.

"Princess Varanda of Vallisto," Stella announced.

Miss Griselda looked Bloom up and down then checked her list. "Let's see ... Yes. Varanda of Vallisto."

"Yeah," Bloom said with a nervous chuckle. "That's me."

Miss Griselda checked her off the list. "You may come in," she said then turned to the girl behind Bloom. "Next!"

Bloom and Stella stepped past Miss Griselda and joined the rest of girls. "Welcome to Alfea!" said Stella.

Once everyone was checked in, Miss Griselda joined the new arrivals in front of the main entrance. She paced in front of them like a drill sergeant barking orders at new recruits.

"Our first rule is our code of behavior," she lectured. "If you break the rules once, you will either get detention or be turned into a frog." Several of the girls glanced at one another and grimaced. "If you break the rules twice, your magic privileges will be suspended." Miss Griselda pointed a bony finger at the girls. "And if you break the rules three times" — she aimed her finger at the front gate — "you will be expelled." The woman smirked at Stella. "Isn't that right, Princess Stella?" She glared at Stella then turned to the others and attempted to smile. Bloom could tell that she didn't smile often. She wasn't very good at it. "Last year, Princess Stella here destroyed the entire potions laboratory when she tried out an unauthorized magic spell. This brings me to the second rule. No unsupervised magic at any time!"

"You really did that?" asked Bloom.

"I was trying to create a new shade of pink," whispered Stella.

"We believe that discipline is the only way to prepare you for the world out there," Griselda continued. "Which brings me to the third rule. Stay away from the Witches of Cloud Tower, no matter what!" She directed their attention to the cluster of dark clouds on the horizon. "We don't have a punishment for that since nothing we could do would be as terrible as what *they* will do to you!"

After her speech, Miss Griselda led them up a wide staircase toward the main building. As the group of girls reached the top, the two main doors swung open and out walked a pleasant-looking older woman. She seemed very prim and proper. Not a gray hair was out of place atop her head. Her kind eyes inspected the new girls.

"Welcome, all," she said with a smile. "I'm Miss Faragonda, your headmistress. I'm an Alfea alumna and a former fairy godmother." She stepped closer and surveyed the group closer. "This year we have quite a wonderful class!"

With Griselda at her side, Miss Faragonda led everyone into the main building. As soon as they were past the two large doors, they found themselves in a grand entryway. Large columns supported a round balcony that circled the entire room. The walls were adorned with paintings of famous fairies and former students.

"Some of you will fight evil," she said as she walked. "Many of you will go on to grant wishes. And a few of you are princesses who will someday rule your own realms," said Faragonda. The girls followed her to the foot of another grand staircase. "Each of you is unique, and you all have different sources of power and diverse origins. But no matter who you are, our mission is the same. We are here to help each of you become the very best you can be."

"To help each of you become the very best you can be," Stella mocked playfully and giggled. "She really loves saying that."

"Naturally, we expect you to repay us by doing your best at all times," Miss Faragonda instructed.

"Now, ladies." Miss Griselda stepped forward. "It's time to check into your dormitories and meet your roommates."

"Remember, everyone," Miss Faragonda added. "Let's make this a great year! Use every opportunity to connect to your Winx!"

Bloom followed Stella and the rest of the girls as they walked up the main stairs. "It sounds like they prepare you for all kinds of different stuff," said Bloom. "Do you know what you're going to be?"

"Duh," Stella replied. "I'm going to rule the kingdom of Solaria."

Bloom smiled. "Right." The two girls split from the others and headed for the east dormitories. "And what did she mean by connecting to your Winx?" Bloom asked.

"Winx is many things," Stella explained. "It's your source of power, as in your strength and energy, but it's also what guides you. It's your magical identity."

"I think I got it," said Bloom. "Sort of."

"You either have Winx or you don't," said Stella. "And *you* have it!"

Stella found their room assignments on a bulletin board, then led the way down another hallway. "I hope our roommates are more fun than the ones I got last year," she hoped out loud. "Their wardrobes had a monumental lack of color."

Stella located their apartment and opened the door. Bloom was amazed by how beautiful and spacious their new residence was. Huge, fluffy couches and chairs filled the main living area. Flowing curtains draped the entrance to a large balcony overlooking the main courtyard. The apartment was decorated with large tropical plants and furnished with a computer and stereo system.

"This is great," Bloom exclaimed as she set Kiko down on the thick carpet. The little rabbit immediately hopped onto one of the fluffy couches.

Stella walked across the living area and opened another door. "But of course I won't be bunking up close. I ordered a single." Stella opened the door to a huge bedroom with its own balcony, bathroom, and king-sized bed.

"This room is sweet!" Bloom gushed.

"Come on." Stella moved to one of the two bedrooms across the living area. "Let's see what yours looks like."

They opened the door to find a much smaller bedroom. But to Bloom, it seemed just as grand. It had two smaller beds, a large desk built into the wall, and was filled with even more plants. There was so much greenery that Bloom accidentally stepped on a vine that stretched across the floor.

"That hurt!" yelled the large plant.

"Wow!" said Bloom. She had never met a talking plant before. She bent closer to the giant bud in the center of the pot. It seemed to be the plant's head. "I'm sorry."

Two leafy eyes glared up at her. "Watch where you step next time," it said.

Just then, a girl stepped out of the bathroom. She had long brown hair and a lovely dark complexion. "He's my latest creation," she said. "He's cute. Isn't he?"

"Yeah," Bloom replied.

"My theory is that if more plants could talk, deforestation would be dramatically reduced!" She knelt and scratched the plant under what looked like its chin. "It's worth trying, even if it saves just one tree." She stood and extended a hand. "Hi, I'm Flora."

Bloom shook Flora's hand. "I'm Bloom."

Stella nudged Bloom with her elbow. "Bloom!" she whispered.

Bloom totally forgot that she was pretending to be someone else. "Oh, what I meant was ... Bloom is a name I like a lot," she explained, "but it's not *my* name. Actually, my real name is, uh ..." Bloom stepped outside her room and looked at the name on the door. "Varanda from ... uh ... Vallisto. Yup, that's me!"

"Vallisto, fourth world of Magic Realm's upper ring," said a voice from behind. Bloom spun around to see a girl carrying a small, blue suitcase. She was dressed in ultra-modern clothing and had short, purple hair. "Vallisto is renowned for its rich artistic tradition. Its beaches are very popular with tourists."

"Right," said Bloom. "That's...where I'm from."

"Cool," said the girl. "My name's Tecna."

"Nice meeting you," said Bloom.

"Hi, Tecna! I'm Stella."

Tecna smiled and cut her eyes at Stella. "You are quite infamous, Stella."

"That's the word on the street," said a girl standing just inside the front doorway. She also carried a suitcase but had short black hair pulled back into two short pigtails.

"I'm Musa." She pointed to Stella. "Yo, if you plan to blow up more stuff, let us know ahead of time so we can bounce!"

"It was in the name of fashion." Stella crossed her arms and turned her head. "I don't regret it."

"I'm curious," said Tecna. "Were you actually able to create this new shade of pink?"

Stella rolled her eyes. "No," she admitted. "But when I do, it's going to be the official color of Solaria!"

Eeeeeeeeeeeeeeeeee!

The scream came from Bloom's room. The girls ran inside to find the talking plant shaking a very frightened Kiko. The little rabbit dangled upside down as a long vine wrapped around one foot.

"Bad, bad plant!" Flora shouted. "Put him down right now!"

Bloom caught Kiko just as the plant released him. The little bunny turned back and sneered at it. "It's okay," Bloom told Flora. "I bet Kiko tried to eat it. He likes his veggies."

"Are you hungry, little bunny?" Flora scratched the top of Kiko's head. Then she went to a table and grabbed a flowerpot full of dirt and a small sack of seeds. "Here," she said as she sprinkled the seeds over the dirt. They immediately sprouted into four large carrots. "They're organic!"

Kiko licked his lips as Bloom set him down beside the pot. The little rabbit was in heaven.

"Speaking of food," said Stella, "I'm famished."

"I'm starved, too," Flora agreed.

"I have a brilliant idea," said Stella. "Why don't we get out of here and go downtown for pizza?"

"Great idea," said Flora. "Downtown Magix is so much fun!"

"What is it like?" asked Bloom.

"It's fresh!" said Musa.

"You've never been?" asked Tecna.

"No," Bloom replied. "But if we can grab a slice…I'm *so* there!"

Chapter 11

The five girls rode a bus from Alfea to downtown Magix. In the distance, Bloom could see the skyline of a huge city approaching. Everyone knew it was Bloom's first time to Magix, so Stella covered Bloom's eyes as they neared the city. After a bit longer, Bloom felt the bus pull to a stop.

"What do you say?" asked Bloom. "Can I open my eyes now?"

"Almost," said Flora as they carefully led her down the bus steps. They shuffled her forward a bit, and Bloom heard the bus pull away.

"Okay, take a look," said Tecna.

Stella uncovered her eyes.

"What do you think?" asked Musa.

Bloom gazed around at the amazing city. Huge skyscrapers pierced the sky as crazy streets and overpasses wound around them. Cars without wheels hovered just above the ground as they zipped by. Pedestrians dressed in

all different styles of clothes crowded the sidewalks. To Bloom, it looked like a city from the future. However, it was not what she expected.

"To be honest with you," said Bloom, "I'm kind of disappointed!" She pointed to the shiny skyscrapers. "I mean, this is it? Downtown Magix? The most enchanted city in the universe?"

Musa shrugged her shoulders. "Well, what did you expect?"

"I don't know," Bloom replied. "Dragons, unicorns, rainbows, giants, flying brooms…"

"But that's all fairy tale stuff," said Stella. "This is the real world." She pointed to a car as it glided into a parking lot. "What's cool is that everyone here knows magic and they get to use it all the time, for anything they want." The man driving the car leaned out his window and pointed a finger at two parked cars. Magically, the crowded cars slid away from each other, leaving a perfect parking space between them. The man pulled his car in the new spot.

"That was cool," said Bloom.

"Yep," Stella agreed. "And way better than a valet."

"Time for pizza!" announced Flora.

"Yeah, chow time!" Musa agreed.

Stella placed a hand on her stomach. "My stomach's growling."

"Mine, too!" said Tecna.

The girls joked and laughed as they strolled down

the sidewalk and didn't notice a familiar ogre inside a nearby shop.

Knut pawed through the many different pairs of eyeglasses on the rack. If those witches were going to make him wear glasses, at least he could pick out a pair of frames he liked. He snatched up a fluffy pink pair and placed them on his head.

"Now, those frames *really* bring out the pink in your eyes," said the man behind the counter. "Very chic!"

Knut examined his reflection in a mirror. "Are you sure they don't make my nose look too big?"

"Oh, you have a tiny nose for an ogre," the salesman complimented.

Although the salesman continued to flatter him, Knut stopped listening. Instead, his attention shifted to the five young girls walking past the shop window. Two of them looked very familiar.

"Did you see what I just saw?" asked Knut.

"What was that?" asked the salesman.

Knut rubbed his chin. "I'm pretty sure I saw the princess walk by just now."

"Oh, yeah," said the salesman. "I saw them. They looked like a bunch of Alfea students. The new school year started today."

Forgetting he was wearing the pink glasses, Knut rushed out of the shop.

"Hey, get back here, big nose!" yelled the salesman.

As Knut ran down the sidewalk, he reached into his overalls and pulled out a small mobile phone. "I have to call Her Highness. I can't mess up this time!" The ogre dialed the number with his chubby fingers then put the tiny phone to his ear.

"Talk to me," said a girl's voice.

"Your Viciousness?" asked Knut.

"You again!" yelled the girl. "I thought I told you this number was for emergencies only. What is it now?"

"It's about Princess Stella," replied Knut. "I spotted her and her friend in downtown Magix!"

"Downtown?" There was a short pause. "Meet me in Witches Alley right away!" she ordered. "We'll take her scepter, then use its power to finish her off!"

CHAPTER 12

Bloom was stuffed. The pizza in downtown Magix tasted better than any she'd ever eaten. She probably ate too much, but she couldn't help herself. Luckily, Stella informed her that the food in Magix wasn't fattening. Bloom could get used to this kind of diet.

She reached into her pocket and pulled out her mobile phone. Bloom wanted to call her parents and let them know everything was all right. She also couldn't wait to tell them about the amazing things she had seen.

Bloom dialed home but nothing happened. She tried again, but still nothing. She examined the screen and saw that the phone wasn't even getting a signal. "My phone isn't working for some reason."

Tecna held out a hand. "Let me see it," she said. "I love taking these things apart."

Bloom handed her the phone, and with a long fingernail, Tecna popped off the phone's casing. After examining its internal circuitry, she began to laugh.

"What's so funny?" asked Musa.

"This phone is ancient technology," Tecna replied. "It belongs in a museum."

"But it's the newest model," Bloom explained.

Stella leaned over and whispered in Bloom's ear. "On Earth, maybe."

"You need an inter-realm phone to call home," said Musa.

"Right," Tecna agreed. "There's one just down the street." She reassembled Bloom's phone and handed it back. She then pulled out a small, plastic card. "Here, use my calling card."

"Thanks," said Bloom.

She left the pizzeria and walked down the sidewalk. Bloom quickly spotted what looked like a futuristic pay phone inside a clear dome. Luckily, it had the familiar handset and numbers she was used to. Hopefully, that was all Bloom needed to call home. After she inserted the calling card and dialed the number, she was glad to hear her mother's voice on the other end.

"Hello?" asked Mrs. Peters.

"Hi, Mom!" said Bloom. "Everything is great! The school is wonderful, and I'm sharing an apartment with Stella and three other girls!"

"Have you learned any more magic?" her mom asked.

"No, courses start tomorrow morning," Bloom replied. "But don't worry, I'll keep you posted."

Although her mother had more questions, Bloom

became distracted. The ogre Stella had called Knut walked by. *What is he doing here?* Bloom thought. She quickly turned her head so he wouldn't recognize her. Then she watched him lumber down the sidewalk toward the pizzeria. Bloom had to do something.

"Look, Mom, I'm using my friend's phone card, so I really should go," she said. "But I love you, and I'll call you tomorrow night, okay? Bye!"

Bloom hung up the phone and removed the calling card. She stepped out of the booth and took off after the ogre.

Knut had tracked the girls to the pizzeria. He knew that they would be there a while, so he made one final sweep of the area before heading to Witches Alley. When he arrived, he thought he was the first one there. Then Icy stepped out of the shadows. Knut quickly took off the pink glasses and crammed them into his overalls.

"Well?" asked Icy. Her long, white ponytail swayed as she walked.

"I saw Princess Stella and that other girl," Knut reported. "They're with three other girls eating pizza."

"Was she wearing her Solaria ring?" asked Stormy. She stepped out of the shadows and seemed to bring a cold front with her. Her purple boots clicked on the hard pavement.

"I think so," Knut said nervously.

"We have to get that ring!" said Icy.

Darcy was the last to join them in the light. She placed her hands to her temples and her eyes turned white. Her long brown hair fluttered as electricity buzzed around her. "Ladies, I sense an intruder," she said.

"Why don't you split and take care of them?" Icy suggested.

Darcy clapped her hands together and levitated off the ground. She closed her eyes and seemed to shimmer a bit. Then she split into two identical witches. When both Darcys were back on the ground, the real Darcy turned to the decoy. "You know, sometimes I forget how pretty I am." With a snap of her fingers, the real Darcy disappeared in a flash of purple light.

Bloom carefully peeked over some empty garbage cans. She saw the ogre meet up with three teenage girls. They were all dressed in dark colors and wore way too much eye makeup. Bloom had never seen one of the witches from Cloud Tower. But if she had to guess, she would bet they looked like those three.

For a moment, the huge ogre had blocked her view of the witches. Frustrated, Bloom craned her neck, trying to keep an eye on all of them. And if the opportunity arose, she planned to creep closer so she could make out more of their conversation.

Finally, Knut stepped aside. *That's better,* Bloom thought. Once again, she had a perfect view of all three witches.

Suddenly, the back of her neck tingled. She turned to

see the witch with the long brown hair materialize behind her. *That's impossible,* Bloom thought. *I just saw her right there.*

The witch thrust her hands forward and shot two sonic beams at Bloom. *"Electric Booty Kick!"* she yelled.

ZAP!

Bloom crashed through the empty trash cans as she was blasted down the alley. She tumbled over the hard asphalt and rolled to a stop in front of the ogre and the witches.

"Well, hello there," greeted the witch who seemed to be in charge.

CHAPTER 13

"**Who are you?**" asked Bloom as she slowly sat up.

"Who are *we?*" the witch asked with a chuckle.

Knut pointed to each of the witches. "Well, that's Icy, Stormy, and Darcy. No wait, that's a copy of Darcy."

"Shut up, you oaf!" Icy barked. She pointed a finger at the Darcy standing next to her. A small burst of sparkles shot from her fingertip and dissolved the illusion.

"We are witches from Cloud Tower," said Icy.

"And we're seniors," the real Darcy added from behind Bloom. She strutted around Bloom to join the other two.

"Nobody messes with senior witches," said Stormy.

"But if you tell us where your friend Stella is, we might forgive you," said Icy.

"Back off!" Bloom shouted. "I have magic powers!" Bloom thrust an open palm toward the witches, but only a trickle of sparkles emerged. Icy waved it away as if it were a few mosquitoes.

"That poor girl barely has any Winx," said Stormy.

"That is just *so* sad," Icy mocked. "Let me show you what real magic looks like!" She held out her hand and a glowing ball of light formed just above her flat palm. The orb grew as it seemed to draw energy from the air around them. Icy grabbed the glowing sphere then reared back as if she were throwing a baseball. She heaved it at Bloom, and it burst at her feet. *SHING! SHING-SHING! SHING!* Ice crystals jutted up from the ground, forming a sharp cage all around her.

Darcy held out both hands and shot a double blast of sonic waves. *ZAP-ZAAAAP!* The waves vibrated the ice crystals until they exploded. *KA-BAM!* Bloom was sent flying backward.

"Your turn, Stormy!" Icy prompted.

Stormy raised both hands and lightning crashed from the sky. She brought them down and a small tornado appeared in the alley. *WHOOOSH!* It zigzagged toward Bloom until it swept her up and twirled her high into the air. When Bloom neared the second story of a nearby building, the tornado vanished. She had to grab on to a small ledge to keep from falling.

Bloom didn't know what to do. She knew she had magical powers, but she had no idea how to use them. And even if she did, she doubted they would be strong enough to take on one witch, much less three.

"Get down here!" Icy ordered. She sent a burst of blue-white sparkles toward Bloom. Like a giant hand, the glittering cloud slapped her away from the building. Bloom plummeted to the alley floor, crashing into a pile of cardboard boxes.

As Bloom groaned, the witches laughed. "This is so much fun," said Icy, "but I'm quickly running out of patience." She blasted Bloom with tiny ice crystals from her fingertips. "Fairies don't last long on ice!"

The small shards stuck to Bloom's feet and began to form a giant sheet of ice. It crept up her legs until she was completely entombed. Bloom could barely breathe, and the ice was packed so tightly around her, she could hardly move to shiver.

"You better start talking," Icy commanded. "Where is Stella?"

"I'm right here," said Stella. She and the other girls appeared on the other side of the alley.

"Let her go!" Tecna ordered.

Icy laughed. "Yeah, right!" She pointed to the ogre. "Knut! Crush those losers!"

Knut roared and charged the group of girls. The four of them were backed against a wall, but they didn't move. In fact, they didn't even look worried. Just before the ogre was upon them, Stella yelled, "Now, girls!"

They leaped high into the air. *SMACK!* The ogre made a huge dent in the brick wall. As the girls floated, each of them extended the first two fingers on their hands. Then they crossed their hands as if they were forming a giant V. As soon as they made this sign, they began to change.

Bloom had seen Stella change into a fairy once before, and even though she was encased in ice, Bloom was amazed as she watched all *four* girls make the same transformation. Energy washed over each of them, and their clothes magically morphed before her eyes.

Stella's outfit was exchanged with the golden two-piece she had seen before. Flora was now dressed in a glittering pink dress shaped like petals from a flower. Musa danced in midair as she sprouted silky wings and wore a shiny red miniskirt and boots. And energy crept over Tecna's body until she was dressed in a sparkling silver jumpsuit, complete with neon fairy wings.

Each of the fairies landed gently beside Bloom. Ready for battle, they glared at the three witches. The ogre slowly stood and prepared to charge again. However, before he got his bearings, Tecna stepped forward.

"Digital Web!" she shouted as she sent a burst of energy flying toward the ogre. Instead of hitting him, it split around him, forming a giant, imprisoning ball of energy.

Musa raised both hands. *"Subwoofer Blast!"* she yelled, and two bursts of light shot from her hands. They landed on each side of the trapped ogre and formed giant speakers. The enormous subwoofers blasted Knut with deafening sonic energy. *BA-BOOM-BA-BOOM-BA-BOOM!*

"Ivy Rope!" cried Flora as she blew onto her open palms.

Golden seeds materialized from her hands and wisped toward the ogre's feet. When they hit the ground, a magical vine sprouted and grabbed Knut's leg. Soon, the long vine wrapped completely around him. With a simple motion of one finger, Flora had the vine toss the ogre onto the roof of a nearby building.

"What a useless ogre," Icy said as she watched him fly above her. She snarled and turned her attention back to the four girls. "Put on your sweaters, ladies. It's about to get piercing cold!" She spread her arms wide and a swarm of ice darts shot toward the fairies.

"Everybody behind me," said Tecna. The others dashed behind her as she raised one arm. "*Firewall!*" she cried, and a green energy shield formed in front of them. *KRASH-KRINK-KRUNCH!* The hundreds of shards shattered as they struck the magical screen.

"I have a news flash for you, fairies!" said Stormy. She thrust out one hand and lightning erupted from her palm. *KKKKKRAKLE!* It blasted against the shield and smashed it to bits. The four fairies flew backward and tumbled down the alley.

"Now I'll hit them with the *Ice Coffin*," said Icy. She raised her hands and began to draw energy from the air.

Stella got to her feet and quickly took off her ring. She tossed it above her. "*Sun Power!*" she yelled.

The ring flashed brightly as it transformed into the long scepter. Stella caught it and held it up against the block of ice imprisoning Bloom.

WHOOOOOOSH! Two fat clouds of frozen mist shot from Icy's hands. They began to cover everything in the alley as they were billowing right for the fairies.

"*Vacatus Imediamentus!*" Stella yelled.

In a flash of golden light, Stella, Flora, Musa, Tecna, and Bloom teleported out of the alley.

CHAPTER 14

Several blocks away, the fairies gathered around a shivering Bloom. Stella knelt beside her. "It's okay," she said. "You could have survived at least another fifteen minutes in that ice."

"It d-d-didn't f-feel like it," Bloom said through chattering teeth.

"You know, Bloom, considering you're from Earth and all, you did outstandingly splendidly!" Stella congratulated her. "You were very brave."

Musa leaned closer. "Stella?"

"Why did you just call her Bloom?" asked Flora, her hands on her hips. "And did you say she was from Earth?"

Stella laughed nervously. "Uh…there might be some minor details we need to fill you in on." She helped Bloom to her feet. "Look, I'll give you the whole scoop on the way to Alfea."

On the bus ride back, Stella told the others all about how she met Bloom. She described Bloom's power and how she was able to help defeat Knut and the ghouls. She also described her plan to have Bloom take Princess Varanda's place at Alfea. Stella finished the story just as they entered the main entrance.

Bloom sighed. "I think I want to tell Miss Faragonda the truth, too."

Stella waved that idea away. "We'll talk about that later," she said. "For now just follow me." She began to move up the main stairway.

"Freeze!" yelled a shrill voice.

Startled, the girls jerked their heads to see Miss Griselda and Miss Faragonda standing just inside the doorway.

"Do you have any idea what time it is?" asked Griselda.

"We were worried about you," said the headmistress, shaking her head. Her usual kind expression was replaced with one of frustration. "I want you to go to bed right now," she ordered. "We'll have a little talk about this tomorrow."

As the girls turned to leave, Miss Griselda grabbed Bloom by the arm. "Hold it right there, Princess Varanda," she ordered. "What *truth* did you want to tell Miss Faragonda?"

The girls froze on the staircase and stared at her. Bloom looked up at them and wondered if this was the last time she would see them. "Well," Bloom said as she nervously wrung her hands. "I'm not Varanda, and I'm not from Vallisto."

"You lied to us?" Griselda asked with wide eyes. "You've broken *two* rules in one day!"

69

"She certainly did," Miss Faragonda agreed. She put a hand to Bloom's chin and walked a circle around her, as if inspecting the girl. "But she must be a magical creature or the barrier would have kept her out of Magix."

Stella ran down the stairs. "Don't blame her," Stella said as she stepped in front of Bloom. "It was all my idea!"

"*That*, I believe," smirked Miss Griselda.

"It's okay, Stella," Bloom said as she stepped around Stella. "My name is Bloom. I'm from Earth."

Griselda's jaw dropped. "Earth? As in planet Earth?" She turned to Miss Faragonda. "How could that be possible?"

The headmistress leaned closer to Bloom and looked into her eyes. "I didn't think there was any magic left on Earth."

"But please don't send me back," Bloom pleaded. "I know I belong here. This is the most amazing place with the most awesome people ever!"

Miss Griselda pointed a finger toward her. "Well, you must be punished and turned into something slimy!"

"Hold on." Miss Faragonda kindly pushed Griselda's hand down. "It took a lot of courage for Bloom to speak up as she did." She smiled at the young girl. "I think that we should give her a chance. We could let her stay and take Princess Varanda's spot."

"What?" asked Griselda.

The headmistress gave Bloom a pat on the head. "Now, go to bed," she instructed. "And try to be good, okay?"

"Yes, ma'am!" all the girls said in unison. They spun around and ran up the stairs.

Bloom was in shock as she followed the girls to their apartment. She couldn't believe it. She could stay at Alfea and learn how to be a fairy like the other girls. But best of all, she could be herself!

"It's the first class of the year," said Professor Wizgiz in his high-pitched voice. "A year full of great potential and limitless possibilities. And that, dear girls, is what metamorphosis is all about!" The short elf paced between the rows of desks in his classroom.

Bloom had been instructed by some odd teachers before. It seemed as if all teachers had their different little quirks and mannerisms that made them unique. However, all of Bloom's former teachers had at least been human. Professor Wizgiz was an elf who was barely as tall as the students' desks. He seemed very nice, however, and even playful. And since he was dressed all in green, he looked more like a leprechaun than an elf.

"Metamorphosis is the art of changing how you appear," Wizgiz said as he leaped onto his desk at the front of the classroom. "Once you master it, you can turn into anything you like. Let me give you a little preview." He plopped down on the edge of the desk, his legs dangling. "Look at me now, an average elf." He pushed back his sleeves. "All right? Look at me now!"

The professor grabbed one cheek and stretched it far away from his face. When he let go, it snapped back into place and his head vibrated. He reached up, grabbed his big green hat, and threw it to the side. By the time the hat hit the floor, Professor Wizgiz had transformed into Miss Griselda.

The entire class gasped.

"Pretty scary, huh?" asked Wizgiz's voice coming from Miss Griselda's scowling mouth.

The classroom full of girls looked at one another then burst into applause. Miss Griselda raised a finger, and the room silenced.

"The beauty of magic is that you can always go back to being you." Miss Griselda adjusted her glasses, then shrank to the floor. Bloom craned her neck to see past the girls in front of her. Suddenly, Professor Wizgiz leaped back onto his desk. He slapped his green hat onto his elfish head and took a bow.

As the girls applauded once more, the professor hopped down and walked down the center aisle. "For now, we have to start with the basics," he announced. "We'll warm up with a very simple exercise — changing your hair color." He snapped his fingers and silver hand mirrors appeared in front of every girl in the glass. "You should all be able to breeze through this one."

Stella grabbed her mirror and immediately began

adjusting her hair. Bloom reached out and took hold of her own floating mirror.

"Look at your reflection in the mirror," Wizgiz instructed. "Focus your Winx and go. Try to change it."

Bloom glanced around the classroom and saw the other girls change the color of their hair. They simply closed their eyes and their hair turned to shades of orange, blue, and green. Bloom gazed at her reflection and concentrated on turning her hair purple like Tecna's. She squinched her eyes shut but when she opened them again, her hair was still red. She tried again, concentrating harder, but still nothing. Bloom sighed and placed her mirror on her desk.

Professor Wizgiz hopped onto her desk. "Bloom, it's a little early to fall behind," he warned. He picked up the mirror and handed it back to her. "It looks as if you have a lot of homework to do."

Bloom did much better in the rest of her classes. She learned some defensive spells in her Enchantment class. She correctly mixed all her assigned recipes in Potions 101. She even surprised herself by answering a question correctly in Magix History. However, she was still troubled by her failure in Professor Wizgiz's class.

After school, she sat on her bed and stared into her mirror. No matter how hard she concentrated, she just couldn't change her hair color. "I was the only one who couldn't do it," Bloom said as she flung the mirror onto the bed.

"You'll get it," said Stella. "You just have to practice."

Bloom sighed and grabbed the mirror again. "Okay, I

can do this," she said. "It's like when I had to learn to high jump back in Gardenia."

"That's the right attitude," Stella encouraged. "And before you know it, you'll be growing fairy wings!"

"I sure hope so," said Bloom. She concentrated on making her hair bright pink. Once again...nothing.

"Let's try this." Stella sat beside her. "Think about the best hair day you've ever had. Concentrate on how happy you were and use that feeling to change your hair color."

It was worth a shot. Bloom closed her eyes and imagined having the best hair day ever. Then, all of a sudden, she could feel it working! She actually felt some of her hair move. Unfortunately, when she opened her eyes, she realized that her bangs were now sticking straight up. She looked as if she had horns.

"Great," she said, pointing to her head. "This is what I end up with?"

"I'm just trying to help you, okay?" said Stella. "You're a bigger project than I thought." Stella got up and crossed her arms. "You just have to take it day by day."

Bloom put down the mirror and flopped back on the bed. "I hope tomorrow's better." She pushed down her pointy bangs.

"Well, the learning curve for the first semester at a new school is quite steep," said Stella.

That night, the entire dining hall was in full chatter as usual. Bloom sat with her friends, but she didn't say much. She was worried that she really didn't fit in at Alfea. Her friends were much further along than she was. They could even grow fairy wings and fight off witches. Bloom thought that maybe the powers she had used that day in the forest had been a fluke. Maybe she should have stayed on Earth after all.

The girls continued to eat and socialize as they sat at rows of long dinner tables. Miss Faragonda and the teachers ate at a table at the head of the large hall. The headmistress blotted her lips with her napkin and stood. "Young ladies. Your attention, please." She tapped a glass with the edge of a spoon. The ringing soon had everyone silenced. "I have an exciting announcement to make. As is the Alfea tradition, we'll kick off the new school year with a formal dance."

Several of the first-year girls squealed with excitement. Miss Faragonda had to tap her glass once more to hush the eager crowd. Soon the hall was silent again. "Our back-to-school gala will take place tomorrow night, and our special guests will be the boys from the Red Fountain School for Heroics and Bravery." This brought on more excited discussion, but the girls quickly hushed to hear the rest of the headmistress's speech. "We hope you'll be warm and friendly hostesses and make them feel right at home."

Miss Griselda stood and raised a bony finger. "But not *too* friendly," she warned. "There will be chaperones present and love spells are strictly forbidden!"

Miss Faragonda smiled. "But dancing's encouraged, and

the boys will bring surprise gifts for all. I'm sure you'll have a wonderful time!"

Bloom smiled as the other girls made plans for the dance. The hall buzzed with talk of what to wear and who was coming. She hoped this dance would be just the tension reliever she needed. Her smile broadened as another thought occurred to her — a thought that both excited and terrified her. Would Brandon be there?

CHAPTER 16

High in the ramparts of the Cloud Tower School for Witches, a different announcement was about to be made. The witches gathered in a huge bowl-shaped chamber as they awaited the arrival of their own headmistress. The hushed buzz of conversation echoed off the ribbed walls and jagged fixtures on the ceiling above.

Icy, Darcy, and Stormy sat among the hundreds of girls sent to school to master the dark arts. The three of them were at the top of their class and they knew it. Icy was particularly proud of this fact. She loved the way the other girls feared yet respected them. She wondered why Headmistress Griffin had called for them to assemble. Icy hoped it wasn't in her honor. If it were, she would have picked out something more dastardly to wear.

When Cloud Tower's headmistress stepped onto the balcony overlooking the audience below, she didn't need to tap a glass. Immediately, the entire assembly stopped their chatter. The scowl on the woman's stark complexion could be seen by all. Even from a great distance, her black eyes seemed to pierce the soul of anyone who fell under her gaze. Icy hoped she would look that wickedly evil someday.

"Young witches, I hope your first day of school was full of nastiness and troublemaking," said the headmistress. "But now I have an exciting announcement." She paused to survey her minions below. "We're going to kick off the year with a very wicked schoolwide competition." There was a slight rumble of approval from the crowd. "The objective is simple and cruel. It is to sabotage Alfea's precious back-to-school dance."

Icy smiled as girls clapped and cheered around her. Headmistress Griffin raised a hand, and the chamber was silent immediately. "Everyone is welcome to suggest ideas," she said. "The winners will receive a gift certificate to Aberzombie & Witch." There came more sounds of approval as the headmistress continued. "It's up to you to dream up a way to turn their celebration into a catastrophe. I encourage you to be as witchy as possible. May the worst witch win!"

Icy smiled as her head was flooded with horrific ideas. However, one plan rose above the others.

"I think this is the perfect chance to get Stella's ring," Darcy suggested.

"You read my mind," Icy hissed.

"But the point is to sabotage their party," said Stormy.

Icy laughed. "Then we'll kill two birds with one stone!"

*   *   *

The next day after school, Bloom's friends tried on different gowns for the big dance. Bloom hadn't packed anything formal, but her friends offered to let her borrow something of theirs. Unfortunately, none of their dresses were really her. And even though she was beginning to worry, she had fun watching the other girls show off their fancy gowns.

"A party is only as good as what you wear to it," Stella said as she dug through her closet. "And this will be an *excellent* party." The other girls watched as she spun around with a gorgeous burnt-orange gown. "Behold! An Eyewink Wizrahi!"

The dress was very sleek, backless, and had a high collar that connected the straps. "I maxed out the credit card Daddy gave me, but I didn't have a choice, it was calling out to me." Stella dramatically reached a hand forward. "Buy me! Buy me, please!"

"It's so definitely you," said Musa. She wore her crimson, kimono-style gown. It sported an elaborately high collar with long velvet sleeves and flowing cuffs.

Stella held her hand against the sparkling fabric. "My ring really doesn't go with this, though."

"I wish we could just use magic to create outfits," said Flora. Her corseted, strapless gown was simpler than the others, but it wasn't less elegant. Huge, pink petals adorned the front, and thin, green vines spiraled around her arms.

"Yeah, it took me forever to find this thing," said

80

Tecna. Her ultramodern, short skirt was wrapped by a floor-length, sleeveless jacket. A violet collar jutted over the back of her head, and her coat was pinned closed with a sparkling purple brooch.

"It's so interesting," said Musa. "Where did you get it, Mars?"

Tecna ran a hand over the shimmering, blue fabric. "I researched it thoroughly. This is *the* latest in fabric technology," said Tecna. "It won't wrinkle!"

Bloom sighed. "I'm worried. Brandon will be there, and I have nothing to wear." She still wore her jeans and T-shirt.

"Pa-lease," Stella said waving a dismissing hand. "No friend of mine is going to feel apparel shame. There's a simple solution to any fashion dilemma."

Everyone looked at one another and smiled. "Shopping!"

CHAPTER 17

Stella and the others took Bloom on a whirlwind tour of the finest dress shops in downtown Magix. Bloom couldn't believe there were so many great stores. Some had clothes that were the same style as those on Earth. But most of them carried strange and elaborate designs that Bloom had never seen before.

They took her to store after store but nothing seemed right. Finally, Bloom found a beautiful azure gown. It fell off one shoulder and had an open midriff. Everyone thought it was perfect.

"Too perfect!" Stella agreed.

"I know!" Bloom spun around to look in the mirror. Then she grabbed the dangling price tag. "Too expensive!"

Stella pulled a credit card out of her purse. "I'll pay for it," she offered.

"Stella!" said Flora. "You maxed it out, remember?"

Bloom returned to the dressing room. "It's okay," she said. She glanced at the large clock outside. It was getting late, and she could tell that her friends were anxious to get back and start preparing for the dance. "You guys can go back and get ready. I'll keep looking."

"Are you sure?" asked Flora.

"You can text me if you need me," said Stella.

"Your probability of success is still high," said Tecna.

"I'll be fine," said Bloom. "Go get ready, I'll see you later."

The girls returned to the bus stop as Bloom changed out of the expensive dress. She then left the store and began searching for a clothing store that wasn't quite as upscale.

"With my allowance and these expensive stores, the only way I'll find a dress is with some serious luck," she said as she continued down the sidewalk. Then she spotted a huge red sign in a shop window. "Or with a sale!"

Bloom dashed inside and headed straight for the sale racks. She flipped through discounted gowns and rummaged through bins of bargain dresses. Finally, she found one with a large red tag reading 80% OFF. The dress was a beautiful cobalt blue and its fabric was light and glistening. Unfortunately, it was a size too big and its style was a bit frumpy. Bloom didn't care, though. She had found a dress she could afford. Plus, there was nothing wrong with it that a pair of scissors and a spool of thread couldn't fix.

Bloom paid for the dress and jogged back to the bus stop. She had only an hour before the dance started. She would have to work fast.

*　　*　　*

Icy, Darcy, and Stormy trekked up the stairs leading to the highest point of Cloud Tower. Crackling torches lit the way as they marched to the headmistress's office. Darcy and Stormy seemed a bit worried. Icy wasn't concerned; she was excited. They were three of Miss Griffin's favorite witches. They couldn't be in trouble. Their summons to her office could only be good news.

When they entered the large room, the headmistress sat behind her massive desk. It seemed even taller because it stood on a raised platform. Miss Griffin sat behind it in a chair that looked more like a throne than a piece of office furniture. Her large book of spells sat on a pedestal behind her.

"I received a number of proposals for ways to ruin the Alfea dance," said Headmistress Griffin. "But none were as disgusting as yours!" Darcy and Stormy cringed. "A repulsive idea! Revolting! Despicable!" Miss Griffin continued. "In other words, it's the best!" She slapped the paper onto the desk and stood. "Congratulations. You're abominable."

Icy smiled while Darcy and Stormy sighed with relief. "That's sweet," said Icy. "Thank you."

"It's just the thing to spoil their fun," Miss Griffin sneered.

"You won't be disappointed," said Darcy.

"It'll be a night full of wickedness," Stormy hissed.

"Not to mention upchucking and projectile vomiting," Icy added. Everyone, including the evil headmistress, cackled with laughter.

CHAPTER 18

Back at Alfea, Bloom burst through her bedroom door. Hair dryers, makeup kits, combs, and curlers littered the apartment. Apparently, her friends had finished getting ready and had already gone downstairs. With the exception of Kiko and a few of Flora's more intelligent plants, Bloom had the place to herself.

"I found a great dress, Kiko!" she said as she threw the dress onto her bed. "It just needs a little work."

Bloom rummaged through the nearby desk for the supplies needed to make the necessary alterations. She found a needle and spool of blue thread, but there was something else she needed. "There has to be a pair of scissors somewhere," she said as she ran to her closet and began tossing things over her head.

She sighed and returned to the bed. Kiko was trying to help. The little rabbit gnawed at the edge of the dress. Bloom scratched him behind the ears. "Thanks for trying, Kiko." She pulled her hand away and stared at it. "Hey, what's the point of having magic if you can't use it for the simplest things?"

Bloom extended a finger and pointed to the bottom of the dress. She had to have enough Winx to make the small cut she needed. A thin, golden beam shot from her fingertip and began to sear through the thin material. She smiled as the she moved the beam across the dress. She would have it altered in no time.

Suddenly, she heard voices coming from outside her window. They weren't the usual voices she heard out there. These were boys' voices.

Bloom stopped cutting and ran across the room. She pulled back the curtains and peeked outside. Just as she suspected, the Red Fountain boys were arriving. They looked very handsome in their blue uniforms and long, flowing capes. She scanned the crowd until she found who she was looking for.

"Brandon's here, Kiko," she squealed. "He looks so cute!"

Kiko replied in an unusually loud squeal, and Bloom smelled smoke. She spun around to see that her dress and bed were smoldering. She dashed to the bed just as the smoking material burst into small flames. "Oh, no!" she cried as she grabbed her pillow and began slapping at the fire.

Once the flames were out, Bloom opened the window to clear out the thick smoke. Her new dress was singed a bit, but her bedspread sustained the worst of the damage.

She hoped one of the other girls could clean up the mess with one of their spells. She supposed she should leave the magic to the rest of her friends for now.

Bloom ran downstairs in search of scissors. The dance had already begun, and she had barely started her alterations. As long as she was finished in time to squeeze in at least one dance with Brandon, she'd be happy.

Bloom could hear the music and laughter coming from the main hall. She hoped no one would see her as she made her way to the basement door. She opened the door then quickly slipped inside. After turning on the dim light, she descended the long staircase.

"I didn't know we'd be walking," a distant voice said. "These heels pinch my feet."

"Don't even start your witching, Darcy," said another voice. It sounded closer. "Once we get that ring, we'll so rule! We'll take chariots everywhere."

Bloom recognized those voices. They belonged to those three evil witches from Cloud Tower. What were *they* doing here?

CHAPTER 19

As Bloom crept down the dark stairs, she saw three flashlight beams dance on the walls below. She stopped and listened as the three familiar voices grew louder.

"Please tell me we're almost there," Darcy whined.

"You tell me," Stormy replied. "You have the map to these secret tunnels."

"Oh, right," said Darcy. A paper rustled. "We *are* almost there."

"Hey! Who stepped on my foot?" barked Icy.

As the lights grew brighter and their voices louder, Bloom carefully tiptoed up the stairs. So far, they hadn't seen her in the darkness. Bloom dashed through the doorway and quietly shut the door behind her. Too bad it didn't have a lock. If it did, she'd lock those wicked witches down in the basement.

Bloom ran away from the door and hid behind a nearby column. As soon as she was concealed, she heard the basement door creak open.

"Now, where are those Red Fountain gifts?" asked Icy.
"I sense we're very close," Stormy whispered. "Go straight
ahead and make a right."

Bloom took a chance and peeked around the column.
Luckily, the three witches were walking in the opposite
direction, their backs to her.

What do they want with the gifts? Bloom thought.

Once they had turned down another hallway, Bloom
took off after them. She ran as quietly as she could until
she reached the corner. She poked her head around and
saw the three witches standing in front of a large closet.

"Here they are," whispered Stormy as she opened the
door. Inside the closet was a large green chest, trimmed in
gold. The three witches knelt in front of it.

"This school is so cheesy," Darcy whispered. "I don't
even know why the Red Fountain boys want to hang out
with these losers."

"Well, it's not like we'd want to socialize with those
nerds, anyway," said Icy. "We have better things to do."

Bloom ducked behind the wall just as Icy spun around.
She held her breath, hoping that she hadn't been spotted.

"All right, Darcy," Icy said after a long pause. "Locate
the ring."

"I have the perfect spell for that," said Darcy.

Bloom dared to peek around the corner once more. She
saw Darcy wave her hands in front of her. "*When this spell
is cast, show us the past,*" said Darcy.

Bloom watched as purple shafts of light flashed from

Darcy's eyes. They shone on the nearby wall like a film projector. "*Show us where she put it*," Darcy chanted. "*Show us where it is. Show us where to find it.*"

Soon, an image of Stella and Bloom appeared. It was like watching a home movie, except there had been no camera in Stella's room earlier that day. Bloom watched as Stella took off her Solaria ring and opened a small jewelry box. The magical playback cut to a close-up of Stella's hand pulling out a golden seashell case. She placed the ring inside the shell and then returned it to the jewelry box.

"Oh, no," Bloom whispered.

Icy laughed. "This will be like taking candy from a fairy." She pointed at Stormy. "Your turn. Let's check out the gifts."

Stormy waved her hands over the trunk. "Open!" The trunk obeyed her command. Packed inside were lots of golden eggs. Each egg was the size of an ostrich egg and covered with an orange, diamond-shaped pattern.

Darcy grabbed one and twisted it as if it were a plastic Easter egg. When she removed the top, the egg burst in her hands. It changed to hundreds of magical, golden butterflies. "Enchanted little eggs," Darcy sneered. "How sweet."

"They'll be the most memorable gifts these losers ever receive," said Icy. She raised a glowing finger into the air. "*Turn the enchanted into the cursed,*" she chanted. "*Give them a bite that will make them puke first!*"

Darcy raised a finger over the trunk. It began to glow as well. *"The eggs will hatch and snake-rats will appear."*

Stormy added her glowing finger to the mix. *"And spread panic, nausea, and terrible fear."*

The three witches pointed at the eggs in unison. Beams of light shot from their fingertips and splayed over the eggs. Their diamond designs morphed into snakelike swirls.

That's awful, Bloom thought. She was so flabbergasted that she almost didn't duck in time when the witches turned her way. They walked past the corner, toward the wall on the opposite side of the hallway.

"When we're done with them," said Icy, "those precious princesses won't know what bit them!"

"I can't wait to see the snake-rats," Stormy added.

"How long will it take for the fairies to start puking?" asked Icy.

"One bite, and it'll only be a matter of seconds," Darcy replied.

They laughed as they reached the wall. Icy raised a hand and a swirling portal appeared there. The three girls stepped through and the churning gateway disappeared behind them.

"I have to warn the girls," said Bloom as she ran toward the main hall.

When she zipped through the main doors, she saw the great hall transformed for the dance. The dining tables were gone and elaborate streamers adorned the walls. All the Alfea girls looked very elegant in their colorful ball gowns. They mingled and danced with the handsomely dressed boys from Red Fountain.

Bloom tried not to worry about being underdressed. After all, this was an emergency. However, she still crouched as she snaked through the crowd. The less people that noticed her, the better. Especially if one of those people were...

"Brandon!" Bloom yipped as she suddenly found herself face-to-face with him.

"Hi, Bloom," he said. "I was looking for you."

Bloom's stomach tightened and her face warmed. "You were?" she asked.

"Sure," he said with a smile. "Would you like to dance?"

"Yeah, for sure," Bloom replied. Then she spotted Stella and the others. "In a minute, okay?" She sprinted toward her friends.

Bloom was completely, totally, and utterly embarrassed. In the midst of all the well-dressed girls, Brandon had to see her in plain jeans and a T-shirt. But then again, he didn't seem to notice. He even asked her to dance! Bloom shook her head as she turned her attention back to the emergency at hand. She would have to be embarrassed now and excited later. "Girls!" she shouted as she ran up to her friends.

"Bloom!" said Stella.

"What took you so long?" asked Tecna.

"Where's your dress?" asked Flora.

"The witches are here," Bloom explained. "They have a plan to sabotage the dance!"

Bloom led them to a deserted corner of the hall. She explained how the witches came through a secret tunnel and how she had followed them.

"What are they going to do?" asked Stella.

"I heard them casting some freaky spell on the gifts the boys are going to give us," said Bloom. "It had something to do with snake-rats."

"Snake-rats?" asked Tecna. "Let me consult my database." She held out her palm and a wide beam of light emerged. Strange writing scrolled through the air in front of her. "Snake-rats: venomous swamp creatures," Tecna read. "Can cause projectile vomiting with one bite. Gross!" The text was replaced by a holographic image of a furry lizard with a mouth full of fangs. Sharp, sawtooth scales ran down its spine.

"Eeww," said Stella. "I bet those witches are just jealous of us. They wish they had a chance with the Red Fountain boys."

"Well, actually the witches are not after the boys at all," Bloom explained. "They're really after your ring."

"We have to do something," said Flora.

"It's cool," said Musa. "We can handle it. We'll just go to the dorm and get the ring right now."

"Uh, too late!" said Flora. "Look!" She pointed to a large crowd forming on the dance floor. Everyone gathered closer as Sky and Timmy, two of the boys who visited Bloom's house, carried the large chest to the center of the hall.

CHAPTER 20

"**We hope you** like the gifts we brought you," said Sky. He opened the trunk to reveal all the eggs packed in neat little rows.

"I don't see any snake-rats," said Musa. The girls watched the action from their secluded corner of the hall.

"The spell said they'd hatch from *inside* the eggs," Bloom explained.

"We need a counterspell and fast!" said Stella. "Come on! Let's form a ring. Focus your Winx." The girls grabbed one another's hands and stood in a small circle. "Now let's link our powers together," said Stella.

"*Let all the dark magic be reversed,*" the girls chanted. "*Make the eggs like they were before they were cursed.*"

Bloom concentrated until she could feel the power rise inside of her. She opened her eyes and saw a golden glow forming inside the circle. The luminescent ball burst into a thousand tiny flickers of light. Then the cloud of sparkles flowed away from them and toward the center of the hall.

It hovered close to the floor as it snaked around the legs of the partygoers. When it reached the chest, the cloud shrouded the eggs and the orange swirl designs were transformed back to their original diamond shapes.

Sky reached into the box just as the glow faded. He pulled out an egg and handed it to a nearby girl. She opened it and it transformed into golden butterflies.

"Wow!" said the girl.

Soon, all the girls received an egg and the entire hall was filled with magical butterflies.

Stella leaned against the wall and let out a deep breath. "Spells are exhausting!"

Sky stepped away from the chest and approached the group of girls. "This one's for you, Stella." He handed her one of the golden eggs.

"How cute," said Stella. "An enchanted little egg, thank you."

"Let me see it," said Musa as she playfully snatched it out of her hand. She turned to Flora. "Remember that Tundra spell in this issue of *Teen Fairy?*"

Flora smiled. "I sure do. I can use it to give those witches a taste of their own magic." Musa gave her the egg. Flora held it in one hand as she passed the other over it. "Let's see, my Tundarian is a little rusty," said Flora.

"Just go for it, girl," encouraged Musa.

"*Shmrorongurabu . . .*" Flora chanted.

"What was all of that?" asked Bloom.

"Yeah?" asked Sky.

Flora giggled. "That was the Spell of the Month from *Teen Fairy* magazine." She pointed to Bloom. "Hey, you should go get into your dress now."

"Unbelievable!" Icy yelled. She was so angry that a small patch of the enchanted bamboo forest suddenly iced over. The rigid stalks shattered and crumbled, revealing the three witches hiding behind them.

"They counterspelled us!" Darcy growled.

"How dare those freshman counterspell *us*?" said Icy. She peered through the large windows in the great hall. Golden butterflies flew over the happy partygoers.

"Let's go get them!" Stormy yelled.

"No," said Icy. "We have to stay focused. We're here to get the Solaria ring. And once we do, we'll be the most powerful witches in all the eight realms!"

Bloom ran into her room. With Musa's scissors in hand, she went to work on her dress. "I did my first spell ever, Kiko," she said as she trimmed the gown. "It was so cool!"

Suddenly, Kiko chirped an alarm. Bloom looked up to see a small green box float past her bedroom door.

"That's Stella's jewelry box!" Bloom yelled. "Her ring is in there!" The box floated out of the their apartment and down the hallway. Bloom dashed after it. "I am not going to let them get it. No way!"

Bloom chased the flying box out the school's main doorway and into the dark courtyard. Just as she gained on it, the box trembled, then snapped open. The golden sea-shell case flew out of it and the green box dropped to the ground.

"The ring!" Bloom yelled.

Now she chased after the floating seashell. *There has to be a spell for this*, she thought. *Let me think…*

"*One, two, three, come back, ring!*" Bloom yelled. The case continued to fly away. "*Four, five, six, stop that thing!*" It didn't even slow down.

"Boy, was *that* pathetic," said Bloom as she hurried after the ring.

She chased it across the vast lawn as it zipped toward the small bamboo grove near the outside main hall. Just as it was about to disappear into the dark stalks, Bloom leaped as hard as she could. "Gotcha!" she yelled as her hands clasped over the case. She hit the ground hard but smiled in triumph. Her smile faded, however, when the three witches stepped out of the dark bamboo.

"Look, it's that Earth-girl loser!" said Icy. "She thinks she can just walk away with *our* ring!"

As Bloom lay on the ground, the three witches stepped closer. "First, we'll kick her booty," Stormy announced.

"Second, we'll freeze her," Icy added.

"And third, we'll finish her off," threatened Darcy.

Bloom quickly got to her feet as Icy raised her hands high into their. "*Ice Bracelet!*" she yelled and shot a beam of light at Bloom's feet.

ZIP!

The glowing shaft hit the ground and immediately formed a ring of ice around Bloom. The ice crackled as it swirled tighter. When it was almost to her feet, Bloom jumped as hard as she could. She leaped over the ice and landed on dry ground. Before she could completely recover, Darcy stepped forward.

"*Heel of Oblivion*," Darcy yelled as she slammed one foot to the ground. *RRRRRUMBLE!* The earth cracked and a giant chasm stretched from her to Bloom. The ground shook as Bloom fell to her knees. The crack surrounded her, blocking any chance of escape.

"Twist her!" yelled Stormy. The third witch waved her arms above her and a small tornado formed. *SHWOOOOSH!* The twister churned the ground as it crept closer. Bloom backed away until her heel was over the edge of the chasm. She slipped and dropped the golden case as she toppled over the edge. The case landed on the ground above, but Bloom fell into the crack. Luckily, she grabbed the lip of the small gorge with one hand.

Icy extended a hand, and the case floated into the air. It sailed over, and gently landed on her outstretched palm. She stepped toward the dangling Bloom. "There is no escape for you now," she said. Then she glanced at the other two. "May I do the honors?" she asked.

"Of course!" said Stormy with a laugh.

Icy looked down and snarled at Bloom. "You pathetic

Earth girl. How did you even get into this school? You don't have any Winx!"

"You're wrong," Bloom yelled back at her. She struggled to keep her grip. "I do have Winx!"

"No," said Icy as she raised a hand into the air. A sphere of bright light formed in her palm. "I don't think so."

CHAPTER 21

As **Icy prepared** for her final attack, Bloom concentrated. "I'll show you," she said under her breath. "I *do* have Winx. I know it."

Bloom imagined having a great power deep inside her. Then she actually felt an immense burning within. As Icy sent the giant ball of ice hurtling toward her, Bloom imagined that the fire inside her burned so hot that Icy's attack would be melted instantly. Before she knew it, Bloom's imagination had turned to reality. The ice evaporated.

Bloom levitated out of the chasm and felt fire burn over her entire body. She let the flames wash over her as she floated. She felt her old clothes being scorched away and new ones forming. Fire burned long gloves onto her arms, boots onto her feet, and a sparkling blue two-piece outfit over her body. Most important, Bloom felt a tug on her back as a pair of wings sprouted.

She opened her eyes and looked down at herself. "I knew I could do it!" And she had. Bloom was now a fairy.

She turned her attention to the three very surprised witches. "Now, let's see what you're made of!"

"Oh, how cute," said Icy. "You got your fairy wings. Too bad your little outfit can't do your fighting for you." She turned to Darcy. *"Perceptus disorientus."*

Darcy placed both hands against her temples. Suddenly, Bloom's entire world was made of rubber. The ground, the trees, and the buildings all seemed to wobble and gyrate around her.

"I can handle this," Bloom said as she held her head in her hands. "I have to focus. Just focus, Bloom!" She shut her eyes and concentrated. "I got it!" she said as her wings fluttered behind her. She flew high into the air and suddenly, the world was back to normal. Bloom glared down at the witches. "Now you better hand over Stella's ring or you'll face my wrath!"

Icy sneered. "Hey, get a load of that 'tude."

"I *know*," Darcy agreed. "A couple of wings and she thinks she's all that!"

"We're going to teach you a lesson, Earth girl," said Icy, raising her hands high into the air. *"Frozen Prism!"*

Enormous shards of ice burst from the ground. *SHING! SHA-SHING!* They jutted in every direction until they surrounded the flying fairy. Her new wings fluttered madly as she dodged each new crystal. When they seemed to stop, Bloom looked down, but Icy wasn't there.

"Arctic Blast!" said Icy's voice from behind.

Bloom spun around to see the witch's face projecting

out of one of the tall crystals. The face took a deep breath, then blew freezing air at Bloom. *FWOOOOOOOSH!* She tumbled through the air and crashed through the bamboo grove.

As Bloom tried to get her bearings in the dense stalks, she heard Icy's voice. "All right, let's wrap this up with my personal favorite," said Icy. "*Ice Coffin!*"

Bloom couldn't see the attack, but saw the thick stalks freeze around her. *KRACKLE!* With all her might, she soared through the bamboo and away from the approaching sheet of ice. She burst through the other side just as ice enclosed the entire grove.

As Bloom slowly got to her feet, she heard the witches on the other side. "We've got the ring," said Icy. "And the Earth girl is history. We're done here."

Bloom heard a loud whoosh, and she knew that they were gone. Now transformed back into her regular clothes, Bloom stood and dusted off her jeans. She felt both elated and depressed at the same time. She was extremely excited that she had finally grown wings and had become a true fairy. On the other hand, she had let the witches get away with Stella's ring.

"Bloom!" shouted Stella as she and the others ran up to her.

"Where were you?" asked Flora. "Are you okay?"

"Yeah," Bloom replied. "I had to fight the witches, but I got through it."

"You took them on all by yourself?!" asked Stella.

"How did it go?" asked Tecna.

"Not too bad," Bloom replied. "I actually grew wings!"

"That's brill!" said Tecna. "Congratulations!"

"The problem is that now they have Stella's ring." Bloom hung her head. "I couldn't get it from them."

"They don't have it," Flora smirked. "Remember the spell of the month?"

"Yeah, but what did it do?" asked Bloom.

The other girls just looked at one another and laughed.

CHAPTER 22

In their apartment at Cloud Tower, Icy admired the seashell case. "Finally, the ring of Solaria." She put a timid finger on the clasp. Darcy and Stormy leaned closer. "Ultimate power will now be mine," Icy boasted.

She opened the case only to find a golden egg inside. "Why would she keep it in here?" asked Icy. She shook the egg and heard a strange clunking inside. It didn't sound like a ring at all. Icy grabbed the top of the egg and began to twist. Instead of opening, it exploded into a black cloud. The three witches coughed and gagged as the putrid smoke engulfed their room.

"Uhhh, that's disgusting!" Stormy yelled.

"I think I'm going to puke!" Darcy hacked.

When the smoke had cleared, Icy didn't see the ring of Solaria resting on her open palm. Instead, she saw a little black duckling.

"Whoa," said Darcy.

"Mommy!" cried the duck. "Mommy! Mommy!"

Icy dropped the baby duck and stepped back in disgust. The duckling merely jumped onto her shoulder. It kissed her on the cheek with its tiny bill. "Mommy! Mommy! Mommy!"

Stormy and Darcy couldn't help themselves. They covered their mouths, trying to stifle their laughter.

Icy roared with anger. "I'm going to get them for this!"

Back at Alfea, Bloom was almost finished with her gown. She had to cut and sew faster than she ever had before. But after all she had been through, she wasn't going to miss that dance for anything.

When she finally made it to the great hall, the party was still in full swing. She could tell that her dress was a success because of all the stares she received when she made her extremely fashionably late entrance. She had taken a plain bargain dress and turned it into an elegant strapless gown with sheer sleeves and blue ribbon accents.

She quickly found her group of friends. "What do you think?" she asked, giving them a quick twirl.

"I think this will be a fantastic party after all," said Flora.

"So give me the scoop," Bloom inquired. "Did I miss anything good?"

"Let's see," said Flora. "The headmistress asked Musa to sing for the boys. Prince Sky has been flirting with Stella all night, and Brandon asked where you were. Right, Stella?"

"He certainly did!" Stella agreed.

"This has been an amazing day," said Bloom. "I mean, counterspelling the witches and then fighting them. Then I found my Winx and grew wings, and now the party and all!"

"Awesome," said Flora. "What else could you ask for?"

"I can think of something," Stella said with a wide grin. She peered behind Bloom.

Bloom felt a gentle tap on her shoulder. She turned to see Brandon standing in front of her. She felt her stomach tighten and an uncontrollable smile stretch across her face.

"Uh, hi!" she said, trying not to look too nervous.

"You know, you owe me a dance," Brandon said playfully.

"Right...okay," said Bloom.

Brandon took her hand and led her to the dance floor. Bloom was thrilled that a slow song was playing. He held her lightly in his arms, and they danced gracefully.

"So, how do like Alfea?" asked Brandon. He smiled and his blue eyes sparkled.

Bloom sighed and glanced back at her four new friends. They waved and gave her a thumbs-up. "I'm starting to feel right at home!"

CHECK OUT THESE OTHER

TITLES!

Circle of Friends
Dragon Fire
Fairy Insider
Fairy Princess Tales